Frank Felt it happen.

The old coldness crept in, like it used to back when he hurt people for a living. Numbed detachment flowed from his head down to his feet. He felt his face go flat, his eyelids dropping halfway. He straightened, back stiff and hands relaxed at his sides.

Showtime.

Agonist

Published 2016 by Spiral Publishing, Ltd. www.spiralpublishing.net

Book & cover design copyright © 2016 by Jason A. Adams
Cover art copyright © 2016 by Hemul/Dreamstime.com

ISBN-13: 978-0-9908875-5-3
ISBN-10: 0-9908875-5-3
Library of Congress Control Number: 2016921497

For Kari,
who always believes.

AGONIST

JASON A. ADAMS

CHAPTER 1

Frank Powers sat across from Lawrence Bradshaw, watching with a bemused smile as the fat little man squirmed and sweated. The small, cluttered back office already smelled bad enough with the odors from the bar and its patrons. Now the reek of fear-sweat and nervous bowel wafted around as well.

Frank didn't really give a rat's ass about the other man's emotional state. "You sign, you're mine" summed up his feelings nicely.

This place obviously made a decent profit judging by the number of imported beers the bikini-clad barkeeps drew while he'd waited for Lawrence to show up. The house band wasn't bad, either. Even from back in the office they sounded good. Frank tapped his foot in time to a great cover of Slade's "Run Runaway" pounding through the thin walls. Smiling at the apt song, he drained the last of his soda, the watered-down flavor another indicator of pure-bred North American Tightwad.

Across the beat-up chipboard desk, his chubby pigeon picked up a copy of the contract. Put it down. Picked it up again. The way he compulsively rubbed his fingers over his thumbs, he obviously thought Frank was a walking cliché. Frank knew he looked the part. At six-three and two-twenty, he loomed over the other man even when they were both sitting down. Frank wore black jeans and a black silk shirt with silver cufflinks. Heavy black infantry boots. His working uniform.

Frank finally took pity on his prey.

"Look, Lawrence. You can't pretend to be surprised. The contract spelled everything out, and you assured me you understood all two points of it. In return for a small loan of ten grand, you agreed to remit four equal payments, one each quarter."

Frank believed firmly in the two sentence contract. No wiggle room for either party.

He placed a small glass ampoule filled with clear liquid on the desk, then an old-fashioned three-ringed syringe. Caressing the smooth, highly polished brass cylinder, Frank looked at Lawrence, eyebrow raised and smiling serenely.

"Have you ever heard the term *agonist*, Lawrence? I hadn't, until a doctor friend traded me several vials in return for certain services."

Lawrence gazed down at the tiny bottle, brows knitted. At least he stopped fidgeting so damned much. Then his eyes went to the syringe and he flinched as if already feeling the needle.

"Mr. Powers, please, I—"

"Knock it off, Lawrence." Frank hated this part, when they all started puling about hard times. "You're a week late. Being that I'm a generous guy with a heart of gold, you've got until midnight Friday to make your payment. Plus ten percent extra for the aggravation."

He smiled his favorite just-you-and-me-and-aren't-we-reasonable smile. It was a good one. He'd practiced it carefully.

"And Lawrence? You have my contact information. Please don't make *me* come find *you*."

CHAPTER 2

Back on Piedmont and heading for his next customer, Frank chuckled at how an empty tube and a bottle of water could turn into something far more potent in a pigeon's mind. He was getting too old to break legs. Better to let them threaten themselves. He could never be half so scary as someone's imagination.

Light rain fell as wet streets steamed. Frank drove through the dusk out of Buckhead and toward Dunwoody, where a suburban princess owed him for getting her house out of foreclosure. In the sky, heavy bass drumrolls rumbled constantly. This time of year, you could just about set your watch by the daily thunderstorms.

His cell rang in three short beeps. Horace calling from the office. He hit the stereo, piping his assistant's voice over the speakers. Alpine and Ma Bell had a baby. Frank chuckled before speaking.

"Yo, Ace. Whatcha got for me?"

"Hey, Boss! Where you at? Out of Fuckhead already?" Horace came from Stone Mountain and had no use for yuppies and frat boys. "You need to get your ass back here.

I'm staring at fifteen thou' in small bills, sittin' on your desk and waitin' to multiply."

Another bullshit strong-arm gig. Dammit, he'd told Horace a hundred times...

"Who wants what done to who? You know I don't take up-fronts for anything. I'm just a loan office—

"I know. I know that, Boss. But you want to take this one, I guaran-damn-tee you."

Dead air for a space as Horace waited for him to speak, but Frank could be silent as the grave. Finally Horace said something that shook him. Shook him badly, in fact. Chalk one up for the old bastard.

"You remember Yvonne?"

Yvonne Rudabaugh. A one of a kind name for a one of a kind woman. Frank remembered all right. All too well. Yvonne was a train, and he'd been stalled on the tracks. It had taken a lot of PMS—pain, misery, and suffering— before he'd finally learned his lesson and sworn her off a couple of years ago. At least that's what he liked to pretend. Truth was, he swore her off because she up and disappeared one day.

And like any other addict, he still had a few fond memories and the occasional craving.

"Please don't tell me Yvonne wants to hire me." That would be like sending a junkie on a pharmaceutical delivery.

"Oh no. Not that." Horace said, then paused again.

Little shit's enjoying this, Frank thought.

"C'mon, Horace. Give. Don't make me collect from you." An old threat, and an empty one his friend and associate heard at least once a day.

"It's her husband, Boss. He wants you to find her."

Frank hung up without replying and turned around, heading to the Connector and back to his North Druid Hills office.

Husband, eh? Hard to believe. That was a pretty major change for the hard woman he'd known. In his mind, he heard his father's voice, drawling his favorite phrase out with a twinkle in his eye.

A haaaaard woman, Frank. You'll have fun fer a while, then she'll tear you up one side and down the other, boy.

What had the little minx gone and gotten herself into now?

Frank pulled up to the drab, white office building and parked in his usual spot. At eight in the evening, the lot was empty except for a sleek black Lincoln Town Car. Two men leaned on the fender. One smaller, wearing a classic chauffeur cap and coat, the other a hulking brute with slicked black hair and a wide mustache.

The second man stood taller than Frank and half again as wide, wearing a suit that must chafe the hell out his armpits. The big guy locked on to Frank, eyes tracking him like a gunner's sights. Big, but with something happening upstairs. A bodyguard with a brain. Frank ignored both of them.

The building was a simple two-story square block with a dentist, a low-rent lawsuit-happy lawyer, six vacancies, and Powers Contracting Services. Frank kept the place shabby but neat. A card reading *Out at Job Site* taped to the small window set head-high in the heavy steel door, plus the fact he and Horace always kept the door locked, kept any would-be customers from entering.

Frank took a deep breath, opened the door, and walked in.

Horace wore his usual straw cowpoke hat, brim curled tightly at the sides. The bandanna was green today. He never changed hats, but each day he wrapped it in a different color.

He sat at a large metal desk, the kind of thing you'd see marked down at an office salvage place, which is where he'd found it three years ago when he opened up shop as an independent. The desk held only a computer and telephone.

And a plain manila envelope with a wad of banknotes peeping out.

The scene took Frank back to when he and Horace had worked as collectors and enforcers for various groups on a purely contract basis, which was how he'd met Yvonne.

On the wall opposite, beside a door marked KEEP OUT: HIGH VOLTAGE, a large rectangular block made of Styrofoam and straw hung, covered by a sheet with a man-sized silhouette target. Several knives were stuck in the target's chest and neck, and the handle of a screwdriver jutted from where the target's eye would be. Horace loved flingin' his things, as he put it, and had once been the champeen tomahawker of North Georgia.

He didn't know if his friend was world-class or not, but if he ever pissed Horace off, Frank would make sure he stood at least thirty yards away.

The visitor's chair was an uncomfortable old metal-framed job with a sagging seat, designed to discourage any visitor from staying for long. In it sat a tall, thin, and distinguished-looking gentleman in an expensive grey suit, as relaxed as if it were a plush chaise lounge. He had silver hair, not yet gone to white. His eyes were a piercing sky blue. Frank couldn't see his face, but he could smell some sort of musky cologne wafting off his guest.

The old fellow rose, extended a hand lined with veins and age spots but with no trace of a tremble, and inclined his head slightly.

"How do you do, Mr. Powers?" he said. "My name is Quentin LaRouche. I believe you know my wife, Yvonne." It wasn't a question, and while LaRouche seemed genial enough, he wasn't smiling. His voice was smooth. Cultured. The voice of the genteel old South.

Frank had heard plenty of phony accents over the years. He'd gotten very good at picking up on them, a requirement when tracking people down who don't want to be found.

LaRouche's wasn't bad at all.

It wasn't easy to erase all traces of South Boston, but his guest almost had it. It helped that his chosen fakery also had a lack of Rs. *Powuhs*. Why the hell would Yvonne marry a creep like this?

Never mind, not his business. Not anymore.

"I know her," Frank said. "Or at least I did once upon a time. What happened to her?"

"She is missing," his guest said. "For a week now. She went out to meet some friends, and never arrived."

"Did she drive herself?"

"Yes. Her car was found outside a deserted warehouse near the airport."

"Have you called the cops? Filed a missing person report?"

LaRouche sighed. "There are reasons I am not at liberty to involve the authorities, Mr. Powers. I wish to handle this matter privately, as far as possible."

Yvonne, Yvonne. What are you mixed up in this time?

Frank said, "Okay, tell me. Who would be after Yvonne? Or is it you they're after and just using her?"

The thin man leaned forward slightly, hawk's eyes focused on Frank's own. "My wife speaks quite highly of you. She says you are very professional. And very good at finding people. May I trust your discretion, Mr. Powers? Completely and without reservation?"

Frank stared back with the same intensity. "Depends, Mr. LaRouche. How much are you paying and what am I likely up against?"

LaRouche nodded, apparently satisfied with the answer. Frank had passed the honesty test.

"I will pay you two hundred thousand dollars for her safe return. Half now, which is yours no matter the outcome, for your time and trouble. The other half when she is safely home."

Frank caught Horace's gaze as his eyebrows rose. Two hundred grand to fetch a runaway?

"As far as the opposition, they are...well, not exactly old family men, if you understand," LaRouche said. "Somewhere above the typical street gang, but not well established in the upper circles of our business."

"And what is your business?" Frank asked.

LaRouche pursed his thin lips, considering. "We deal in, let us say, recreation. We provide our clients with products or people to help them forget their miseries for a brief time."

"Drugs and hookers," Frank said. "Why not just say so up front?"

"As you say, Mr. Powers," LaRouche replied. "A crass way to put it, but accurate enough. Our clientele wishes to keep names and details out of the newspapers and off the Internet. We are very exclusive, very discreet, and very well compensated."

"Okay," Frank said. "So how about Yvonne? What's her place in all this?"

"Yvonne is my business manager, as well as my wife. She handles most of the dealings with clients. I work more with our suppliers and employees."

"Makes sense," Frank said. "She was always a charmer." He could see her now. Low cut dress, ankle-breaker heels, folds and waves of coppery hair cascading down her back—

Stop it. That was years ago. Plus, things didn't end well between them. Still, though, *this* guy? What the hell did he have that made him so much better than...

Knock it off, Whiny.

He shook his head, trying to get Yvonne the woman out of his mind. She was Yvonne the target now. "So do you have any ideas who I should start with?"

LaRouche stood and fished a card out of his pocket, passing the small rectangle to Frank.

"I would start here. Check with Marcus Kaplan, one of the security men. Not one of mine, but somebody Yvonne deals with regularly. He can get you in touch with someone who may have information."

Frank took the object, noting that it wasn't a business card, but an advertising leaflet for The Jaguar, one of the more upscale "Gentleman's Clubs." A fancy way of saying a fancy strip joint. He'd heard the girls were *very* friendly. If you had the cash, anyway.

Frank walked to the copier and pilfered a blank sheet of paper. He grabbed a pen from the jumble Horace kept in an hourglass Coca-Cola glass and wrote two sentences.

In return for $200,000 plus expenses, Frank Powers will find and deliver one Yvonne Rudabaugh LaRouche to Quentin LaRouche. Half the payment remittable on contract agreement, balance due on delivery.

He scrawled his signature at the bottom and held the pen to LaRouche, who read the contract over and smiled.

"Very succinct, Mr. Powers. I applaud you." He added his own name below Frank's, then pulled a banded stack of hundred-dollar bills from his jacket and handed it over. "You may take the envelope for expense money. Let me know if you need more."

The two men shook hands, and LaRouche left. The old man's card stuck out from the band around the topmost cash bundle. Frank stuffed the loose bills in his pocket and grabbed the envelope. He pulled out a handful of notes and handed them to Horace.

"Christmas come early this year," he said, fanning the hundreds. Far more intelligent than his hokey demeanor suggested, Horace let Frank do the talking with clients most of the time but filed away everything he heard.

He, Frank, and Yvonne had been a great team once. Horace was the best partner he could ask for, but Frank still missed his old flame.

His thoughts must have been on his face. He caught Horace staring at him. His old friend still had a smirk, but his look was as soft as it ever got.

"You gonna be okay with this, Boss?"

"Sure, Ace. It's just a job, right?" Not the biggest pile of bullshit he'd ever shoveled, but big enough that Horace could smell it.

"You take care of yourself, dude," Horace said. "I mean it. Don't go gettin' yer head blowed off. Or your heart yanked out again."

Frank sucked in air, and let it drain away.

"No promises, but I'll do my best. Hold the fort 'til I get back, Hoss."

CHAPTER 3

Twenty minutes later, Frank parked in front of a garish black and gold building. A large LED screen promised the sexiest girls, the strongest drinks, the finest cuisine, blah blah blah. Lawrence Bradshaw's place all over again, only with better paint and lighting.

He dodged a dark blue Crown Vic on his way to the door, scowling at the thin man behind the wheel. The driver hadn't even looked his way. With the dark aviator shades, the guy probably hadn't even seen him. Who wears sunglasses for a nighttime drive? His cop radar tingled, but cops at strip joints were pretty much a given on a busy night.

He walked in and found a gigantic ape of a guy at the cover window beside a closed door with blackout glass for a window. "Twenty bucks," he said when Frank approached.

Frank sized him up, noting biceps bigger than his thigh, the shirt straining over massive pecs, the bald head, the gold earrings and heavy necklace gleaming against blue-black skin. Then he had it.

"Willie Peterson," he said. "You played defense for the Falcons a few years ago, right? How's the knee these days?"

"Better," Peterson said. "Still bad enough to keep me on the sidelines. You goin' in or what?"

"Maybe. My name's Frank Powers. I'm here looking for a guy named Kaplan. Know him?" Frank drew a fifty from his pocket, creased it down the middle, and tapped it on the counter.

Peterson looked from Frank's face to the bill and back again. Then he held out a hand the size of a dinner plate. Frank slid the bill to him.

"Powers," Peterson said. "You helped a brother of mine out of a tight spot. He said you treated him fair." He smiled a little. "He also said you were a mean mother to cross."

They chatted football and security for a while, relaxed and easy. Peterson seemed like an okay guy, and Frank hoped he wasn't involved. One bad knee was enough for anyone.

Finally, Frank looked at his watch, then up at Peterson, eyebrows raised. The big man took the hint, reaching for the phone. "Kaplan's in back. He's working door security on the girls' dressing room today. I'll ring back and tell him you're cool."

Peterson reached under the counter and Frank heard a low buzz from the door. He walked through and into the full blast of bass-heavy noise, the typical throbbing beat of skin bars everywhere.

For early evening on a Wednesday, the place was crowded. Scantily-clad waitresses scooted through the crowd, expertly fending off drunken hands and ignoring catcalls. On the three stages, dancers were doing their thing in various states of undress, all wearing garter belts stuffed with dollar bills and a few larger notes. Frank didn't see any red hair, so they didn't interest him much.

He waited for the song to end, figuring the naked blonde was done with her show. She took one last twirl around the pole, smiled and waved to the drooling crowd, and stepped down as the DJ called, "Let's hear it for Candy!"

Sheesh. Candy? Really?

Frank followed her at a discreet distance as she walked toward a bead curtain in rainbow colors under a sign reading, "Keep Out! Your Thumbs Will Thank You."

He gave the stripper a minute to disappear down the hall, then brushed through the hanging wooden beads. Immediately he came face to face with a shorter man. Kaplan, he presumed.

Kaplan stood a little less than six feet, his eyes on a level with Frank's neck. He wasn't broad, but rather had the whipcord build of a dancer. Or someone into martial arts. His movements were relaxed, but precise. His eyes fixed on Frank's.

"You Powers?" he said.

"I'm Powers," Frank replied. "Mind if I ask a few questions?" Another creased fifty appeared in his right hand, tapping his left palm.

Kaplan didn't glance at the money, just kept his eyes on Frank's. "About what? And who you asking for?"

"I'm looking for a woman. Red hair. Thirty-four years old. Five-eight. She goes by Yvonne."

Kaplan's face revealed nothing. "I see a lot of redheads in here. None that old, though. Can't help you." He started to turn away, but Frank caught his shoulder.

"The name Quentin LaRouche ring any bells?"

Kaplan stopped, then slowly rotated back to face Frank.

"I know the name, but I don't know the man," he said. "What about him?"

"I'm trying to help him find someone."

"Why's LaRouche need help? He recruits girls from all the clubs."

"Then you know Yvonne," Frank said. "She's his business manager. My guess is you've seen her fairly recently and that's why he told me to start with you."

A second fifty joined the first.

"Yeah, I know her. She's the one who talks our girls into leaving us for her bigshot boss. Promises 'em more money, better clients, all the usual shit."

"Any of them ever leave and come back to work here?"

"Sometimes they come back, sometimes not." Kaplan paused a moment, then went on. "The ones that do come back never talk about their time with him. All they say is he hires 'entertainers' that aren't allowed to say no to clients. Ever."

Kaplan stayed silent for a minute, then turned back down the hall. "Come on," he said. "Let's find somewhere to talk."

They walked back through an open dressing area. Young silicone-enhanced women were changing into or out of various bikinis, negligees, and other outfits. One was even pulling on a pair of Daisy Dukes and a flannel shirt. Frank ignored them and they ignored him. He and Kaplan stepped through another door into a cramped office with a filing cabinet, a safe, and a cheap brass umbrella stand holding half a dozen baseball bats.

Kaplan closed the door and sat behind the desk. He held out his hand and Frank gave him the bills.

"I've seen Yvonne," he said. "She was in here three weeks ago, delivering some...ah...refreshments for the girls. Heroin, coke, speed, whatever they want. I don't like it, but everyone buys their own hell, you know?"

Frank knew very well. Usually he fronted the down payments.

"Anyone with her?" he asked.

"Just Boris. A big Slav who's been watching her back lately."

"Anything unusual about the visit?"

"Not really," Kaplan said. "She was pissed off at someone. I heard her bitching 'em out on her cell phone. But she's always hacked off about something or somebody."

Tell me about it.

"Catch a name?" Frank said.

"No names. Not people, anyway. I heard her say something about meeting up at a place called Mojo. Sounded like she was renting a house."

Mojo was a pizza joint in Oakhurst, an inner city neighborhood that had gone from Crack Central to gentrified sterility over the past few years. He and Yvonne used to hang out there way back when. Possibilities...

"Thank you for your time," Frank said, and slid a card to Kaplan. "Call me if you see Yvonne again, would you? There's another hundred in it for you." Kaplan took the card and said nothing, just sat there as Frank turned to leave the room.

Before he got to the door, Kaplan said, "Hey, Powers."

Frank turned, eyebrows raised, waiting.

"One of the girls who went to work for LaRouche turned up dead last month."

"Overdose?" Frank asked.

"Could be," Kaplan said. "Autopsy report said her veins were full of junk. But I'd say it was the way someone bashed her head in. After raping her a bunch of times, from what the autopsy showed. Some kid was riding his bike through a construction site up around Piedmont Park, found what was left of her and called the cops."

Frank said nothing, just let him talk. Kaplan was no longer looking at him. His eyes wandered to the wall, unfocused.

"She went by Savannah, but her real name was Lisa Hall. She was no angel, none of us are, but she was a sweet kid. Just trying to make a living. She didn't deserve what she got."

"Any idea who took her out?"

"I don't know," Kaplan went quiet for a minute, then said very softly, "She called me a few days before she was found. I was busy and let it go to voicemail. Never took the time to call her back."

He stared at the wall a few more seconds, then turned and faced Frank, face set and hard. "If she was involved in whatever you find, you take care of her payback. Do that, and you don't owe me a dime." He took a business card and a pen from one of the desk's drawers, scribbled quickly, and handed it over.

Frank looked at the back of the card, at the phone number written there. Most likely a pay-as-you-go cell phone.

Frank wasn't surprised by Kaplan's request. People like Marcus Kaplan, Peterson, the girls—hell, people like Frank and Horace—looked after their own. Folks outside respectable society made their own families and watched out for each other.

He nodded once, and left without another word.

CHAPTER 4

Another thirty minutes found Frank walking down a weathered sidewalk, past old bungalows with new cars parked out front, toward a loud and crowded pizza bar with a neon sign over the door. Mojo was spelled out in humming red and yellow, the letters curved and artsy. Frank missed the days when this had been an old black man's barbershop and the streets were gritty and honest.

He'd spent many a night in Mojo with Yvonne, laughing and happy. Later, he'd spent time at the greasy bar pouring his heart out to Horace, at the same time pouring whiskey and beer down his throat.

That was how he learned heartache's a sponge that soaks alcohol in. You can't drown your sorrows, but you can water them and help them grow.

He stepped inside, found an empty barstool, ordered a slice and a seltzer. While he waited he looked around, seeing nothing but expensive clothes, artfully messy hair, and oily beards. What was the world coming to?

His pizza arrived and he ate slowly, savoring the taste and the memories. At least the food hadn't changed.

He thought about where to look next. Thought about the past. Thought about pleasures and pains and regrets. Thought about all the times he'd come back here, hoping.

As if his thoughts held magic, a hand fell on his shoulder and a husky, feminine voice said, "Hello, stranger."

A jolt went through Frank's chest. He turned and there she was. The long red curls were gone, replaced with a short, brunette pixie cut. Garishly scarlet lips curved in a smile. Dark eyebrows, thick and full, rode over eyelids dusted with violet. More makeup than he'd ever seen on her.

"Hello, Yvonne," he finally said. "Someone's looking for you."

She chuckled. "I suppose you mean Quentin?"

He was a sucker for that laugh, God help him.

She sat beside him and ordered pizza and beer. She wore yoga pants and a long pink t-shirt with a wide gold belt, clothes that showed off her curves to great effect. Not bad, but he preferred the black pants and silk blouses he remembered. Between the clothes, the hair, and the face-paint, Yvonne looked nothing like her usual self. She fit right in with the yuppies and hipsters.

Who'd have thought it possible?

"So why doesn't your, er, *husband* know where you are?" Frank asked.

"I think I like the way you say husband. Sounds like you don't approve." She turned to him, smiling a little. "How long did it take you, Frank? An hour? And most of that driving? Do you really think someone like him couldn't find me just as easily?"

"What's the deal, Yvie? And why the costume?"

"You don't like it?" She smiled at him, stretching her arms over her head, pulling the knit material tightly over breasts unencumbered by a bra. She was no bony diet freak. She was fit and luscious, with excellent padding in all the right places.

Frank forced his eyes back to her face, and she smiled again. Enjoying the effect she still had on him.

"If you aren't hiding from your husband, then who are you hiding from?"

Yvonne sighed, then relaxed and went from vixen to serious. "What did Quentin tell you about his business?"

"Pharmaceuticals and escorts," Frank said. "He made it sound like his clients are pretty highbrow."

"The highest. But it's not just dope and nookie. Quentin is also supplying guns and muscle to certain very important people. More important than he is, for sure."

"And?" Frank said.

"And he's ambitious. And he wanted me to grease a few wheels." She grimaced. "I won't tell you how he wanted them greased. Let's just say I wasn't interested in helping."

"So why did he let you leave, then? You said you think he could find you."

"He let me leave because I know his business. He can't just come after me himself, not if he doesn't want the cops and FBI to know what I know. Even if he kills me, they'll get enough to put him under the foundations of the jail."

They ate in silence for a while, Frank thinking and Yvonne waiting. Finally, Frank wiped his mouth on a bright orange napkin.

"He knew about me because of you. What did you tell him?"

Yvonne rubbed his shoulder. "I talked a lot about you.

Quentin doesn't use his own people for collection or troubleshooting. He likes to hire outsiders. No worries about personal problems or friendships getting in the way. I wanted him to think of you first if anything happened to me."

"I'm touched," Frank said. "Especially considering that I haven't seen you since you snuck out on me without saying goodbye three years ago. At least I've been in your thoughts."

He saw her wince and felt a little guilty. Just a little, though.

"Now tell me what I'm supposed to do," he said. "Quentin gave me a pretty big chunk of change to haul you back to him."

"No he didn't," Yvonne said, her eyes not quite meeting his. "He paid you to make it look like he was trying to find me."

"Come again?" Frank said.

"From what I hear, he's putting it out that I insulted his clients by refusing their tender embraces. He's making it look like I'm to be found, brought back, punished severely, and sent right back to them."

"Why would he do that?" Frank asked.

"Saving face is part of it, but I think what he mainly wants is a distraction." Yvonne leaned closer to him. Then scent of her perfume, combined with the aroma of her skin, meant Frank nearly missed what she whispered in his ear.

"He's looking to take over the whole Atlanta vice trade. He wants to control all the clubs, all the street girls and private escorts, everything. Plus the muscle that keeps things running smooth."

"You think he can do it?" he asked. She leaned even

closer. Frank felt her breasts brush his shoulder, and tried not to notice.

"Let's get out of here," she whispered, her breath tickling his ear. "I don't want to talk out in the open like this."

He dropped some cash on the bar, then stood and held his hand to Yvonne. She flowed to her feet, as graceful as always, and led him to the door, still holding his fingers. A table full of college kids winked and gave him a thumbs-up as they walked by. He ignored them and stepped out to the sidewalk, brushing past a short, thin guy in dark aviator sunglasses. He looked familiar...

Nah. Probably just someone he remembered from this place or the U-Joint bar across the road.

"Where we going?" he asked.

"A safe place," she said. "My cousin has a townhouse a few blocks down. She's in Italy for the summer, so we'll have privacy."

Frank certainly hoped so. He let her lead the way, enjoying the movement of her back, legs, and derriere. He was no fool, but he wasn't blind. And she was definitely worth watching as she walked.

They went south for a quarter mile or so, to one of the newer townhouse blocks that had gone up along with the local property taxes. Frank counted doors as they entered the community, and Yvonne stopped at the third on the right. He repeated the count to himself four times to set it in his memory. He'd never be able to find it otherwise. The townhouses were all the same. Clean, uniform, spotless. Pale red brick not yet weathered. Shiny new faux-antique porch lights. Probably three hundred large for the smallest.

No character at all. Frank preferred the mosquito-infested bog that used to be here.

Yvonne used a shiny new key to unlock the door and he followed her in. A small foyer floored with dark, shining oak opened into an ultra-modern kitchen area full of gleaming stainless-steel appliances. Through an arched opening on the far wall, Frank could see a living room beyond. White carpet, white furniture that probably came from Ikea, tasteful Monet prints on the walls. A fireplace free of ash and soot. The place was straight out of a magazine.

A really boring magazine.

"No security alarm?" Frank said, noticing how Yvonne wasn't in a hurry to punch numbers into the ubiquitous blinking keypad beside the door. Horace thought they were hilarious, almost as funny as people believing alarms kept their stuff safe.

So did Frank, but he never said. Better to let folks believe people like him couldn't invade their privacy.

"Not anymore," Yvonne said, smiling sweetly.

She sat on a stool at the granite-topped bar between the kitchen and the larger room beyond. Her eyes traveled over his body, and he returned the scrutiny.

"How's Horace these days?" she asked.

"He's himself," Frank said, sitting beside her. "He's a useless little shit I need to replace."

Yvonne laughed again. Frank enjoyed the way her body moved when she laughed. The way her...

Down, boy. Down.

"How long have you been saying that? Eight years?" Yvonne said, smiling. A warm smile, full of knowing memory. "How about your brother? Talk to him lately?"

"Bill? Last I heard he was out in Nevada someplace, still trying to save the world." He looked her over, noting the toned arms and legs. "What about you? Still kickboxing?"

"A little. Enough to keep in shape. I don't do matches anymore, though. Not enough time for full-on training." She grinned. "Why? Wanna spar?"

Frank laughed. "Hell, no. I'm an old man now. Besides, you could always take me six times out of ten."

"More like nine times," she said, laughing herself.

Frank sat on the stool beside Yvonne's, feeling time contract. It was always that way with her. They both slipped into old roles like comfortable pajamas. He wrenched his mind back to business.

"I want to catch up with you, Yvie, but right now I need to talk to you about work. What do you know about a stripper named Savannah?"

Her shoulders slumped a little, and she turned away, the barstool rotating smoothly. "I don't know exactly what happened, or why."

Frank heard something unexpected in her voice. Something like guilt.

She faced him then, her eyes open and full of real regret.

"Quentin gets new flesh all the time. I found out he's hooking them on heroin or meth, whatever they like too much to refuse. Then he sends them to his friends."

The way she said 'friends' made her opinion clear.

"I delivered drugs and found new girls for him, and I can't undo that. All I could do was leave when I realized what was really going on.

"Savannah went to one of the new ones. A bigshot named Kulish. Russian or Polish or something, one of the main fences for Eastern European sex slaves." She shuddered a little. "Quentin calls them kittenskies. What happened to her?"

"She's dead," Frank said. "Someone caved in her skull and dumped her in an empty lot."

Yvonne closed her eyes. "I'm sorry," she said quietly. "I wish..."

She broke off, shook her head, a quick jerk back and forth. Clearing her mental etch-a-sketch. "Let's not talk any more about trouble right now, Frank. Let's relax, take a break, and get back to it later."

She got up, headed straight for a cabinet over the sink, and started pulling down bottles of clear and amber liquid. "You want something stronger than water?"

"Depends," he said. "What's the plan for the next few hours?"

Yvonne poured something golden and powerful smelling into two glasses, added ice, then turned and walked toward him. Her eyes sparkled and her lips shone. She handed him one of the glasses. She ran her fingers along his jaw to the nape of his neck, then up through his hair. She straddled his lap and leaned in, her lips so close to his face he could feel their heat. Her voice was low and husky as she told him exactly what her plans were.

Shit.

He drained his glass in one quick swallow and dropped it to the floor.

CHAPTER 5

In a fine old home several miles away, a phone rang. An antique baroque item made of red Bakelite and gilt-plated metal. The phone sat on an imported, illegal teak table. The table sat in the corner of a large and lavishly furnished den. Oil paintings of nude women centuries dead lined the walls. Thick camel-hair rugs and the hides of near-extinct mammals covered the floor. Light fell on phone and corpse alike, cast by an enormous crystal chandelier made before Napoleon moved to Elba.

A hand plucked up the receiver. A hand covered with pale skin, parchment-like and spotted with age, but steady and strong. The long fingers wrapped around the barrel and brought it up. A voice said one word. "Yes?"

Silence as the hand's owner listened. Then a short reply. "I see. A pity. Bring the other one to the usual place and leave a note. Call me when you have them."

The receiver clicked back into its cradle.

CHAPTER 6

Frank and Yvonne lay together on a scattering of couch and chair cushions. A trail of clothing led from the kitchen to the living room. A rich, thick aroma of shared pleasures filled the air.

Yvonne stroked Frank's chest, then slid her hand lower, squeezing lightly. He groaned and pulled her hand away. His few remaining hormones tried to rally to the cause, but without much success. She hadn't changed a bit.

"Sorry, Yvie," he said. "The troops need to fall back for a little R&R."

Her lips curled upward, puffy and moist. She sighed, a long, languid exhalation, and snuggled against him. Their sweat mingled, the salty tang just another ingredient in the organic haze that filled the room.

He wrapped an arm around her, stroking her smooth back as he stared upward, unable to relax. His work brain, no longer held at bay by his smaller brain, back in gear. Thoughts of criminals and dead strippers ran through his mind.

Things were deeper than he'd first thought.

He should thank Yvonne for the good time and take her back home. He was a loan shark, not a crusader, and he didn't know anyone involved on a personal level, present company excluded.

Present company was also married to the one who'd hired him.

He told himself it was only curiosity.

Frank gave her a little shake. "What can you tell me about LaRouche and Kulish? Are they partners, or do they just have mutual interests?"

"Mmmm," she mumbled drowsily against his chest. "Not now, sugar. You've worn me out."

"I'm serious, Yvie. I need to know what's going on."

She propped herself on an elbow. "You're kidding. You want to talk business at a time like this?"

"You're in trouble, honeybunch. I might be too." He sat up, wincing a little as sore muscles protested. "If LaRouche finds out I'm sampling the delivery, he won't be happy."

She giggled. "Quentin doesn't care about me, except as window dressing. And as a good business agent, I suppose." The mirth drained away and her expression hardened. "Besides, I'm not going back there."

"Why not?"

"Because it could have been me in that empty lot." She shuddered a little. "Quentin used to be happy with what he had. The people he dealt with in the beginning all had genteel vices and attitudes."

"Like who?"

"Politicians, lawyers, high-class businessmen and women," she said. "People who wanted friendly entertainment and a little something to relax. Now it's all about using the drugs and sex to get more of what he wants, instead of only supplying simple pleasures."

The doorbell rang then. After midnight. At a door to a supposedly empty townhouse.

"Expecting someone?" Frank asked.

"No one knows I'm here," she said. "I only come in or leave when I know the neighbors are gone."

She got up and padded to the door, her naked body like a moving work of art. She glanced through the peephole, then shrugged. "No one there."

She slid the chain, cracked the door, and peeked out. She stiffened. "Frank, you need to see this. Now."

Something in her voice set off an alarm in his head. He got up and strode quickly to her side. He peered through the narrow gap between the door and the frame.

Lying on the doorstep was a straw hat with a tightly curled brim and a green bandanna. Cold washed through him, and his gut clenched with a sudden and heavy dose of adrenaline. He looked around the parking spaces, but all were empty except for a blue sedan. The thin, business-suited driver had just stepped out and was walking down the sidewalk away from Yvonne's place, coffee in hand.

Frank knelt and yanked the hat in. There was a slip of paper tucked in the bandanna. He pulled it free and unfolded it. The note held only one line, block capital letters written in blue pen.

3975 JONESBORO ROAD

"What does it say?" Yvonne asked, leaning over his shoulder.

"It's an address," he said, handing the paper to her. "South of the Perimeter, I think. Industrial area, which makes sense. It'll be dead this time of night."

Bad choice of words.

"I told you he could find me." She hugged herself, shivering.

Frank stood and backtracked, gathering his clothes and quickly pulling them on. "Someone followed me. I wasn't watching for a tail. Someone obviously expected me to find you."

He looked down at Yvonne's stretch pants and pink cotton shirt, still piled on the floor. "Got anything more suited to rough and tumble?"

"Why? What are we going to do?"

"Get my friend back," Frank said. "I doubt LaRouche will be there. Probably just a few goons."

Yvonne shivered again, but the fear left her eyes, replaced with sparkling excitement.

She went to another room, a bedroom he supposed, and came back five minutes later, stripped of the last of her make-believe. She wore sturdy black cotton pants, a long-sleeved white oxford shirt, and a tight black leather vest. A pair of knee high black leather boots with four-inch heels completed her ensemble.

She looked good, like herself at last. Most people wouldn't know what she could do in an outfit like that.

Frank did, and smiled. Old times and old memories.

"Let's go," he said.

CHAPTER 7

THEY TOOK YVONNE'S CAR, A TINY RED MIATA. SHE DROVE and didn't waste any time. The streets were as free of traffic as they ever were in Atlanta, so they took a chance on the outerbelt.

The chance paid off, and half an hour after seeing Horace's crown, they pulled into a cluster of shabby buildings, a collection of old factories and warehouses. Most with broken windows and rusty gates chained shut. Street numbers were painted on the sides in yard-high spraypaint, and they found 3975 toward the back of the complex.

The gate stood open. A harsh glow came through a grimy window and around the doorjamb.

A beat up mid-eighties Ford pickup truck—complete with rusty brush guards, silver silhouettes of nude women on the mudflaps, and a rollbar with a gigantic rebel flag— sat near the door. Gwinnett County plates. Probably a couple of rednecks who were completely badass, as long as they held the upper hand.

Yvonne killed the engine and coasted quietly to a stop. "What do you think?"

"It's a truck, so can't be more than three. Battered woman work for you?"

She smiled. "Perfect! That's always a fun one. Just be careful of the face, okay?"

They got out and walked to the door, which opened into a receptionist cubicle. Another door led from there to the larger space beyond. It stood open, but the angle was bad, hiding whatever or whoever lurked inside.

Frank grabbed Yvonne's upper arm, and pushed her through into a huge and empty room. Marks on the dusty concrete floor showed where machinery had been removed, but not recently. Beer cans, fast food wrappers, and discarded needles told a story of partiers come and gone.

Against the left wall in a folding metal chair, arms behind him and chained to a heavy pipe, sat Horace. His head hung down and he wasn't moving.

To his right, at a table next to a cooler full of ice and more beer, two tall mulleted men were playing cards. Both wore heavy revolvers at their waists, and two Steyr TMP submachine pistols lay on the table.

The revolvers looked old and worn, the machine guns shiny and new.

They weren't, though. Grease guns like that hadn't been manufactured in over fifteen years, so these were probably from some military warehouse.

A half-dressed woman—no, a half-dressed *kid*—huddled on the floor beside the cooler, shaking and rock-ing. Bruises covered her shoulders and legs. Probably brought along as entertainment.

The two 'necks looked up sharply when Frank dragged a now resisting Yvonne into the room. They moved quickly, standing and grabbing up their machine guns and pointing them toward him.

Yvonne sniffled and whimpered, begging Frank to let her go. He shook her a little, then looked from one goon to the other. "Which one of you is in charge here?"

"Who the hell are you, Bubba?" said the one on the left. "You Powers?" He had long, dirty brown hair. He wore faded blue jeans, shit-kicker boots, and a black, sleeveless t-shirt from a recent Molly Hatchett reunion tour.

"I asked you a question, sonny," Frank replied.

"An' we asked you one back," said the one on the right, waggling his gun. "I reckon since we got these and all you got is a girl, you need to be answerin' first." This one wore an identical outfit, except his shirt showed Nazareth. He was a few years younger than the first, and his eyes kept darting around. From Frank, to Yvonne, to his buddy, to the girl on the floor. He looked quickly away from her, maybe not so tough and heartless as he wanted to appear. The barrel of his gun kept jittering, and his weight shifted from foot to foot. Nerves or drugs, but either way, Frank decided this one was Yvonne's.

"Yeah, I'm Powers," Frank said. "I brought LaRouche's delivery." He pointed to Horace's still form. "I'll trade her for him."

"Maybe you will, and maybe you won't," said the older punk. "Seems to me you ain't in no position to trade. We'll take her, though. We like purty girls, even if they ain't young enough." He smirked and nudged the girl on the floor with a dusty boot toe. She moaned and flinched away.

Yvonne played her part well. Tears streamed down her face as she pulled against Frank's grip. "P-please," she said, a catch in her voice. "D-d-don't leave me here. I'll do—"

"Shut the hell up!" Frank snarled. He dropped her arm, slapped her, and shoved her toward Nazareth.

The idiot did just what Frank hoped. He caught Yvonne, taking his right hand off his gun. He still held the foregrip with his left, but foregrips don't have triggers.

"Hey, man!" he squawked. "There ain't no call for—"

Yvonne let herself be caught, her right arm dropping to her boot, then rising up as if to throw around her savior's neck.

In a flash, a knife hilt appeared under his chin just inside the jawbone. Nazareth's face filled with shock and confusion for a moment, then his eyes rolled upward and his legs collapsed.

"What the hell?" Molly Hatchett yelled, stunned by the sudden violence. He gaped at his comrade, now on the ground in the middle of a slowly spreading crimson pool.

Frank wasted no time. He sprang forward and to the left, planted his rear foot, and smashed his right heel through the side of Molly Hatchett's knee. With a loud crunch of bone, the leg folded inward to the sound of his scream.

The roaring clatter of automatic fire filled the room as all Molly's muscles spasmed. Bullets stitched up the wall to the ceiling and spent casings went everywhere.

Frank snatched the gun from Molly's weakening hands. All the shots had gone wild, thank goodness.

"Move again and I'll gouge your eyes out," Frank said calmly, barely breathing hard.

CHAPTER 8

M OLLY WRITHED ON THE FLOOR, BLUBBERING AND CURSING.
He tried to roll, tried to reach for the pistol at his waist, and
Frank stomped his elbow, evoking more squealing.

The guy was running out of useful joints on his right
side.

"Who do you work for?" Frank asked the crippled
redneck.

"I'll kill you, you sumbitch!"

"I doubt it." Frank used his foot to shove him over on
his back. "I think you want to answer my question. Otherwise this 'purty girl' will start asking."

Yvonne leaned down, grabbed the prone man's boot,
and bent his leg in a normally impossible direction. There
was the sound of shattered bones grinding together and the
punk screamed, arms flailing uselessly.

"The Russian!" he shrieked, his face pale and sweaty.
"Kulish! He calls the shots!"

"He tell you to kill Savannah?"

"Who? You mean that little slut we dumped up in
Midtown? She wouldn't play nice, so we—"

Yvonne pulled his foot straight up. His face went ashen and he drew breath to scream again, but only managed a few weak gasps. Frank reached for her hand, and she dropped the leg.

"Don't hurt him any more, Yvie. Not yet. But watch him. If he tries anything, stab him in the nuts."

"Sure thing," she said, pulling her knife free from the dead guy's chin. It came loose with a sucking sound and she cleaned it on his absurd t-shirt.

She grabbed Frank and kissed him hard and deep. Her pupils dilated and vivid spots of color bloomed high in her cheeks. Same old Yvonne.

"Damn, y'all get a room," said a weak voice from over by the wall. Frank freed his face from Yvonne and grinned broadly.

"Hey, Horace. Glad you're still alive," Yvonne said. She sat down on Molly Hatchett's legs, the blade pressed into his crotch, and he went still. He kept on spluttering outraged threats, but they all ignored him.

Frank gently raised his friend's head, wincing at the livid bruises on his face. Horace's lips were swollen, his left eye was nearly shut, but he still had all his teeth. A lump the size of an egg rose from the back of Horace's head, pushing the hair aside.

"You okay, Ace?" Frank asked.

"Yeah, I'm fine," Horace said. "Fuckers bushwhacked me outside the office. They roughed me up some, but not too bad. Get these damn chains offa me."

Frank went through Molly Hatchett's pockets, finding nothing but a pack of Marlboros, a cell phone, and a wallet with about $300. He found the key to the padlock on the dead man, along with another wallet with about the same amount of cash. Another ring held keys to a couple of vehicles, plus a house key and a fob with the same girlie profile as on the truck's mudflaps.

Nice.

Frank unlocked the chain and helped Horace up. He was a little unsteady, but still managed to walk over and kick Molly Hatchett—Tracie Eversham according to the wallet—hard in the ribs. "Asshole," he said, then spat on him for good measure.

Frank handed Horace one of the machine pistols and told him to shoot Eversham if he tried to get up. Then he and Yvonne stepped over to the girl, still shivering and rocking and silent.

They knelt beside her, and Yvonne gently touched her shoulder. "You okay, honey?"

She raised her head just enough to look at them in turn through wide, glassy eyes. She still didn't speak.

She wore the remains of skin-tight shorts and a gold spandex tube top. A pair of shoes with six inch heels lay a few feet away.

Frank glanced at Yvonne, then put his fingers under the girl's chin and tilted her head up until he could see her whole face. "Do you know Savannah?" he asked quietly.

Her eyes flicked to Horace's prisoner, then she shook her head violently. Still no words.

Yvonne said, "Let me see, honey." She gently worked the young girl's mouth open, revealing a tongue that had been split a half-inch back from its tip. Yvonne looked up at Frank, then back to the shivering kid.

"Which one of them, honey? Which one hurt you?" Yvonne's voice was gentle, but Frank could see her rage in the set of her shoulders and the quiver of her muscles.

Again, that quick flick of the eyes toward Eversham. She raised one skinny arm and pointed. Yvonne started to turn, but Frank caught her shoulder.

"Take care of her," he said. "Get her name, if you can. And take her out to your car."

"What about you?" Yvonne said.

"I need to make a call," Frank said, pulling Eversham's phone out of his pocket.

Twenty minutes later, Eversham sat where Horace had been, chained to the pipe. His head hung down, and he'd gone quiet. Shock, most likely. A nice change from his whining and grousing.

Frank and Horace sat at the card table, drinking beer and playing rummy. The Steyrs were in a gym bag Frank found in the truck, along with two spare clips for each. Yvonne came back inside, alone.

"Someone's pulling up," she said.

"Where's the girl?" Frank asked.

"She's sleeping in my car," Yvonne said. "Her name's Audrey. Quentin hired her the same time he hired Savannah. I thought she looked familiar, but I couldn't tell for sure, you know?"

"Okay," Frank said. "Come on, folks. Time to blow this popsicle stand."

They met the two new arrivals at the door. Kaplan and Peterson stood there, stony and grim. They'd made good time from The Jaguar.

Frank felt he could trust them, and they deserved a chance for payback. Payback for a poor dead girl and another who'd probably never be the same again.

"You sure?" Kaplan said.

"Pretty sure, yeah," Frank said. "There's a girl named Audrey out in the red car. I think she knew Savannah."

Kaplan glanced at Peterson, and the big footballer walked outside. He returned a minute later, carrying Audrey as if she were no heavier than a straw doll. She clung to his neck, her face buried against his shoulder. Weeping now. Long, wracking sobs. Frank had to remind himself he was immune to emotional displays.

"It's Sunset, Kap," the big man said. "She's pretty messed up, body and mind, but I think she'll be okay."

"Do you have somewhere you can take her?" Yvonne asked.

Kaplan nodded. "One of the other ladies will take her in for a while," he said, then gestured toward the chained man. "What about him? Did he know Savannah too?"

"Yeah, he did," Frank said. "He admitted doing the deed, more or less."

Kaplan shook his hand, then Peterson did the same. They both hugged Yvonne, apparently not recognizing LaRouche's procurer.

"Thank you, Miss," Peterson said. "Can't thank you enough."

He and Kaplan looked at Frank, and missed Yvonne's flush.

"We're square," Kaplan said. "More than. If you ever need something I can give, just call."

"Me too," Peterson said. "Now you all best be leaving. Don't worry about the trash; we'll clean it up." They went back inside and closed the door.

Frank glanced at Yvonne's little car. Only two seats. He handed Eversham's keys to Horace.

"You okay to drive, pal?"

"Oh, hell yeah," Horace said. "Gimme my hat and tell me the plan, Boss."

Frank stretched until his back crackled and his sternum popped. "I don't know about you two, but I'm bushed. Who's up for a nice bed at the Marquis? LaRouche is buying."

"I'm in!" Horace and Yvonne chimed in unison.

"Dump the truck somewhere," Frank said. "Then meet us in the lobby. You can even have your own room." He grabbed the old straw topper from Yvonne's floorboard and tossed it to his partner.

Horace jammed the hat over his greying hair. He leered at his two companions, threw Frank a wink, then climbed into the Ford. The engine sputtered, coughed, then came to life. Horace waved as he drove off in a cloud of dust and oily blue exhaust.

"Well?" Frank said, turning to Yvonne. "Ready to go get some sleep?"

She folded herself around him, her body conforming to his in a delightfully liquid way.

"We'll sleep eventually, I'm sure." She ran the tip of her tongue over his lips, then pulled away and walked to her little red car, hips and back swaying.

"Shit," Frank said under his breath, and followed like an obedient puppy.

CHAPTER 9

After a quick stop at Frank's place in Decatur for a change of clothes, they drove the back roads to downtown. Dawn kissed the tops of the taller buildings as they passed the familiar gold lions and pulled into the hotel's parking circle.

Yvonne handed her keys to a valet and they walked inside. Horace slumped in an overstuffed chair, feet kicked out and hat pulled low over his eyes. Frank had to shake him pretty good before he finally stirred.

"'Bout time," he said, jaws cracking in a huge yawn.

The three friends trooped over to a long counter, the heavy gym bag bumping against Frank's legs. He paid cash for two rooms for the night. His lack of a credit card wasn't a problem after he dropped a handsome tip in front of the young cinnamon-skinned clerk. She tried to talk him into showing ID, but another hundred and a salacious wink brought her around.

They took the elevator up to the forty-third floor. Horace looked dead on his feet. He'd tried to make light of everything, but he moved slowly and gingerly. Yvonne made him promise to take some pills she produced, and gave him a careful hug.

"Get some sleep," Frank told him. "We'll meet back up around five this afternoon and go from there." Horace nodded, then unlocked his room and went in.

Frank and Yvonne's room was two doors down, an empty suite between them and Horace. The room had a fantastic view of the skyline that he wasn't the least bit interested in right now.

A large whirlpool tub sat in the corner. Yvonne groaned in delight and started the water running. Frank was ordinarily a shower guy himself, but...

"Want me to scrub your back?" he asked.

Yvonne began removing first his clothes, then her own. "No," she said. "I want you to lick me clean, then you can hold me in your lap after the tub's full."

Frank felt no reluctance, to say the least. In less than a minute, Yvonne lay sprawled on the bed, writhing and moaning as Frank devoured her. She grabbed his hair, pulling him closer as her breath quickened and her hips bucked against him. She stiffened and cried out, forcing his face into her until he couldn't breathe, then she fell back, limp and panting.

A cell phone rang. They both ignored it. The ringing stopped.

Yvonne sat up and rolled Frank onto his back. She kissed him deeply, her tongue dancing over his. She moved lower, her tongue, lips, and teeth teasing all the way down. He sighed and closed his eyes as she took him into her mouth.

The cell phone rang again. They both ignored it.

Frank stopped her before it was too late, picked her up

and carried her to the giant tub. He climbed in and settled her onto his lap. She reached down and guided him in.

They rocked together. Slowly, then faster. Water began to slosh over the rim. Yvonne's legs wrapped around his waist, clenching and relaxing. Frank gripped her ass, lifting and lowering.

The cell phone rang. They both ignored it.

Yvonne bit his shoulder. Hard. Her fingernails dug into his shoulders. She gasped and whimpered, riding him harder and faster. Frank felt the edge, felt himself tipping past the point of no return. He growled as he grabbed her waist, slamming her body down onto his until they both toppled into shuddering, groaning orgasms.

Frank fell back against the wet porcelain, breathing in great heaving gulps. Yvonne draped against him, breathing just as heavily.

He was spent and drowsy. He was pretty sure she'd fallen asleep. Frank hated to move, but he shifted Yvonne's inert form to the side and stood before lifting her from the tub and carrying her to the bed.

He laid her down gently, climbed in beside her, and drew the covers over them both as the morning sun streamed through the gaps in the dark velvet curtains.

The cell phone rang again. The ring tone wasn't his, he finally realized. Shit.

Frank rolled over and fumbled on the floor for his jeans. It was the redneck's phone. Frank brought it up and looked at the screen. The caller ID simply said "Work" with a small (4) beside the word. Four calls with no answer. No doubt whose office would be calling this particular phone so insistently.

Frank highlighted the caller ID, quickly memorized the

number, and hit the green button. He heard one ring, then two, then a voice answered.

"You have not phoned me in three hours. Have you taken care of our problem?"

Good English, in a Slavic accent. Frank hit the speakerphone button.

"What problem would that be, Ivan? Surely you don't mean me."

Silence for five seconds. Ten.

"I take it I do not need to worry about paying Eversham and Pruitt." It wasn't a question.

"Boris," Yvonne mouthed at him. She'd opened her eyes, fully alert, as soon as she heard Frank speaking.

"No, you don't," Frank answered. "But I might need some payment, and I *know* Horace will want a little something for the inconvenience."

Another pause.

"LaRouche's woman, you have her?"

"Maybe," Frank said. "Why does Kulish want her?"

"Who?"

"Nice try, Boris," Frank said. "So what's the deal? Is Kulish willing to pay more than LaRouche for the Rudabaugh woman?"

"Something may be worked out, I am sure," Boris said. "I will call you in one hour with terms."

"No you won't," Frank said. "I'll call you. This evening. Eight o'clock." He disconnected the call and turned to Yvonne. "Hand me my shoes, won't you?"

Yvonne leaned over the edge of the bed, giving Frank an excellent view of her excellent derriere, and came back up with his boots. Frank slipped the right one on, and used it to stomp Eversham's phone into random shards of plastic and electronics.

"Shouldn't be too traceable now," he said.

Yvonne smiled and pulled him back onto the bed.

"What's next?" she asked.

"What's next is you tell me what you know about all this," Frank said. "How much do you know about what Boris is up to? How about Kulish? And your husband?"

Yvonne sighed.

"Would you please stop calling him that?" she said, rolling her eyes. "We never got legally married, so I'm announcing the divorce."

"You sure you don't want to be the little woman anymore?" Frank said, grinning.

Yvonne hit him with a pillow, then climbed onto him. "Just for that..." she said, and then proved he wasn't all that tired after all.

CHAPTER 10

ACROSS TOWN, A PHONE RANG. "YES?" SAID THE ANSWERER, his voice smooth and cultured. An American voice, with a genteel Southern accent.

"You have failed," said the caller. He spoke with a thick Russian accent, but the English was impeccable. "Your men did not deliver this Powers or your woman."

"A minor setback, I assure you," LaRouche said. "I will have both of them for you this evening."

"You sound very confident of that. How will you do this?"

"I have other men, haven't I? One of them tells me he is meeting them tonight. He will send them to one of my clubs, where we'll be waiting. We take them, I give her and Powers to you."

A pause, then the Russian said, "Please make sure that you do. I do not wish to believe you cannot handle such simple matters."

LaRouche forced himself to keep his mouth shut, gritting his teeth. Damned russkie prick. The Soviet Union had been gone for twenty-five years, but Kulish still acted like the *Polkovnik* he no longer was.

"I will call you once we have them well in hand."

CHAPTER 11

AT SEVEN THAT EVENING, FRANK AND HIS COMPANIONS DROVE toward the revitalized and newly-trendy Old Fourth Ward. Yvonne's car had only two seats, so they'd rented a nice Audi A8. It was sedan enough to not attract too much attention, and sports car enough to handle any more exuberant driving that might be called for.

Their eventual destination was Diamond Dogz, yet another strip club, where Yvonne figured Boris would be. Kulish owned and operated the club, where the dancers hailed mostly from old Eastern Bloc countries.

They stopped at a place called Joystick, where a large signboard boasted of good food and cheap prices. Cheap for the Ward, anyhow. Frank figured it would be another skin bar, but it turned out to be a lively joint full of classic 80s arcade games. He grinned as he looked over the vintage consoles. *Time Pilot, Gyruss, Tempest, Dragon's Lair*, even a tabletop *Robotron* machine. Memories of the wasted allowances of his youth.

Simpler games than the one he played now, for sure.

The noise and lights made it impossible to be overheard, and nearly impossible to speak to each other. Frank washed down the last of his burger and they all leaned in close.

"Who's going to be in there, Yvie?" he asked.

"Kulish probably won't be," she said. "He has an office somewhere in Midtown. Boris will most likely be there, though. And a few goons."

"How many?" Horace asked. "And what hardware?"

Yvonne wrinkled her brow, her eyes wandering up and left as she calculated.

"Six or seven, plus the regular bar security," she said. "They probably have handguns. Nine millimeters, most likely."

"What about heavier stuff?" Frank asked, thinking of the Steyrs in the gym bag, currently sitting in the Audi's rear floorboard.

"There may be something there," she said, "but it'll be locked up somewhere. Letting the customers see the illegal firearms is generally bad for business."

"Okay," Frank said, checking his watch. Right at eight. "Let's make the call."

They went outside, where Frank pulled the prepaid cell phone he'd picked up at a handy T-Mobile along the way and dialed the number he'd memorized. There was only one ring before Boris answered.

"Powers, yes?"

"That's right, Boris, You willing to deal for LaRouche's wife? Oh, and the inconvenience tax, of course."

"I have been instructed to accept the original deal, I have the rest of your money from Mr. LaRouche, and I will personally add a bonus for the...ah...inconvenience you speak of."

"Where should I bring her?" Frank asked.

"She will know where to find me, I am sure. I will tell my people you are not to be *inconvenienced* any further. When may I expect you?"

"Twenty minutes," Frank said, and ended the call.

He turned to Yvonne. "Can we trust him?"

"I think so. Watch his minions, though. Some of them don't have any manners."

"How about you, Ace?" Frank asked Horace. "You want to come, or sit it out?"

"Aw hell, Boss," Horace said, grinning. "I ain't lettin' you walk into a room fulla Commies without me. You never was good at watchin' your own back."

Frank clapped him on the shoulder. Yvonne was no slouch in a fight, but he'd feel better with Horace along. The wiry old country boy had grown up gay in Stone Mountain, long before *diversity* was a socially acceptable word. He looked like any other jeans-and-flannel-wearing good ol' boy, but he'd been forced to learn all kinds of ways to fight dirty, usually against several opponents at once. Frank topped him by a head and outweighed him by a hundred pounds, and still wouldn't cross him unless Horace was hog-tied and Frank had a projectile weapon.

"Well, let's do it."

CHAPTER 12

They piled back into the Audi and drove slowly toward Kulish's club. Frank parked in a bank's empty lot, the black sedan lost in a sea of similar vehicles. He memorized the lane and slot. Best to not hunt for the car if they left on the run

Clouds had rolled in while they ate, and a low rumble filled the sky. Yvonne looked up as huge drops of rain began splatting against the glass.

"Perfect timing," she said, smiling.

"Whaddaya mean?" Horace said. "We're gonna get soaked!"

"Exactly." She gave him a coy look as she peeled off her vest. "We're going to be drenched, and all I have is this thin little shirt."

Horace still looked confused, but Frank had played this game with her before.

"Don't worry about it, Ace. Just don't forget to pay attention to the crowd." Frank opened his bag, handed Horace one of the Steyrs, and kept the other for himself.

They ran for the employees' entrance at the rear of the

club, Yvonne a little more slowly than the two men. They paused under a long awning, a weathered bench and sand-filled coffee can full of cigarette and cigar butts marking it as the break area.

Yvonne was truly soaked to the skin, hair plastered to her scalp and around her face. Her pants clung to the curves of thigh and buttock, and the white shirt was transparent where her breasts pressed against the wet fabric.

"How do I look?" she said, laughing as Horace rolled his eyes and Frank drank her in.

"I think we're about to learn the Russian phrase for heart attack," Frank said, and pushed the door open.

Yvonne went in first, then Frank, and finally Horace. They followed her down a narrow hallway, the pleasantly-lit and carpeted corridor at odds with the thumping of the dance music that came through the walls.

She stopped at a larger door, finger to her lips. This door had a window which had been painted over, blacking it out. A black acetate plate with white lettering said simply OFFICE.

Yvonne whispered softly, "Right behind me, guys. They'll look at me, you look at them."

They nodded and pulled their guns around, barrels lowered but hands ready. Yvonne stepped through the door, pulling the tails of the shirt and wringing the water out. This had the effect of drawing it even tighter against her tits, and three big guys in leather jackets and beards locked their eyes on her.

Frank and Horace came in behind her, Horace on the left. They could have been tigers or elephants, and the gobstruck goons still wouldn't have noticed.

Three of them sat in metal-framed chairs; two against

the left wall, one against the right. They were goggling open-mouthed as Yvonne wrung her shirttails, leaning forward and letting the sodden cloth droop. Quite the show.

The fourth man wasn't looking at them. He sat behind a small wooden desk, the dark-stained surface scarred and splintered, but neat. Two trays filled with papers and a generic three-line office phone sat on the otherwise empty surface.

Frank realized the desk wasn't really all that small, it just looked that way compared to the giant sitting behind. He was nearly Horace's height sitting down, and would be a few inches taller than Frank himself when he stood. His chest was massive, as were the hands holding a copy of *Time,* of all things. His face held the crooked nose and raised cheekbones of someone who'd been in his share of fist fights, but the black hair and broad mustache were immaculately groomed.

Frank recognized the larger of the two who'd been waiting by the car when LaRouche hired him. The body-guard with a brain.

It wasn't merely his size, but his presence that dwarfed the room. While the other three stared open-mouthed at Yvonne, he merely glanced up from his magazine.

"Yvonne. Hello. You have gotten wet this evening, yes?"

"Hello, Boris," she said. "I hope you don't think I'm going to come back."

Boris looked Frank and Horace over with mild curiosity, then said something in Russian to his men. Frank couldn't understand the quick words, but the tone was cool. The three minions stood and left the office, their eyes on Yvonne until the door closed behind them.

"Please, there is no need for weapons," Boris said, waving his hand toward Frank's gun. Since he could see nothing close to the big man's hands, Frank relaxed slightly but didn't take his own hand from the Steyr's grip.

"So now what?" Frank asked.

"Sit, sit," their host said, waving to the chairs. "Would you like a beverage? Hard or soft?"

Frank glanced at Yvonne, who looked a little puzzled. "No, thank you," he said. "We won't be here long. We just wanted to let you know Yvonne here is off limits."

"Beyond being somewhat fond of this young lady, I have no interest in Madame LaRouche," Boris said. "I am, however, interested in you, Mr. Powers."

"If this is about that redneck punk Eversham and—"

"Don't be ridiculous," Boris said. "They were street offal. Less than dogs. I would have eventually killed them myself for their crimes."

"But you hired them to take Horace," Frank said. "They were your men."

"Not at all, Mr. Powers. They were LaRouche's men. As his very trusted lieutenant, I was able to ensure it was they who took your friend."

"*You* chose them?" Frank said. "They were useless. Yvonne here could have taken them herself."

"Indeed," Boris said.

Now Frank was good and confused. What the hell was this guy playing at?

"What is it you want, Boris?"

Boris leaned forward, hands clasped on the desk, and gave him a piercing stare. Frank could feel himself being weighed and measured. After a full minute and most of the next had passed, Boris nodded, a quick, short, downward jerk of the chin.

"A phone call was made from Eversham's phone shortly before you answered my call," Boris said. "That first call was to a private mobile phone. This phone is a cheap, uncontracted model sold originally at a local Wal-Mart. At the time, the receiving phone was close to a nightclub where works Marcus Kaplan, a man of my acquaintance."

Frank said nothing. He kept the surprise at bay and put on his best poker face.

"I wonder, Mr. Powers, why that phone was used to place this particular call. I also wonder why Mr. Kaplan and William Peterson left the club in such a hurry afterward."

"How could you know all this?" Frank said. "Unless you have someone at one of the cell phone carriers, that is."

Boris waved his hand, brushing the question aside. "That really is of no importance. The *why* is the thing, I think." He rose and paced behind the desk. Frank's eyes followed him up and up. Ye cats, he was big!

"These two men. They demand...or demanded, I suppose...that part of their payment be the company of young women. LaRouche supplied this, and asked no questions."

Frank saw Yvonne's shoulders tremble.

"Quentin is fucking evil!" she said, her voice low but full of heat. "Women are nothing but a commodity to him. Drugs, guns, human beings...they all might as well be groceries!"

Boris stopped and turned to face Yvonne, eyebrows raised. "But you help him acquire these women, do you not?"

She slumped, cheeks flushing slightly.

"Yes, I did," she said. "I thought it was a straight-up prostitution ring." Her eyes snapped up, defiant. "I don't have a problem with voluntary hooking, but Quentin and Kulish, and *you*, you asshole, you people want slaves!"

Boris' expression didn't change. "I, too, have no issue with women, or men, earning a living how they choose to do so, if it is indeed their own free choice." He looked from Yvonne, to Frank, to Horace, and finally back to Frank. "My people fought long and hard for the freedoms you Americans take for granted, and it infuriates me to see them taken away."

"Yeah, yeah," Horace said. "That's sure nice and all, but what's it got to do with us?"

Boris pointed to Horace. "Horace Arthur Greene. Born June 13 of 1962 in Stone Mountain, Georgia." He turned to Frank, then to Yvonne. "Frank Walton Powers, born August 7 of 1969 in Decatur, Georgia, and Miss Yvonne Irene Rudabaugh, born August 28 of 1982 in Des Moines, Iowa. Do I have it all correct?"

CHAPTER 13

Frank, Horace, and Yvonne sat and stared. Frank wanted to act first, even though he wasn't sure how he should.

"Who are you, Boris?" he asked. "That's not the sort of thing most pimps or dealers usually bother finding out."

Boris smiled. "Indeed not, Mr. Powers. Please, come." He opened his jacket, revealing a dull gray semi-automatic in a shoulder holster. "Remove my gun. Then you may relax a little."

Frank had to admit the guy had guts. Still, if Boris trusted him to take his gun, Frank had to trust Boris not to pop his head off when he got close enough.

"Okay," he said, then stood and raised the barrel of his own gun slightly. "No tricks, now." He leaned forward, and plucked the gun from the holster.

"Now you are armed and I am not," Boris said. He walked slowly to the door, hands down and away from his sides. He cocked an ear toward the door for a moment, then gently eased the lock into place.

"My life is now in your hands," he said in a low voice.

He looked at Yvonne. "You wish to prevent more young girls from dying as did Lisa Hall and many others? I wish that as well."

Frank was finally catching on. "You're not one of Kulish's, are you? Not really."

"I am in LaRouche's organization," Boris said. "But I am neither his nor Kulish's. I am waiting to get close enough to Kulish to end him and all his friends." He still spoke quietly, but passion had come into his voice. His eyes were blazing and intent. "LaRouche, as well. He has shown himself to be no better than the pig he seeks to emulate."

"My name is Andriy Borys Kovalenko. I am a Major in the *Sluzhba zovnishn'oyi rozvidky Ukrayiny*, Ukraine Foreign Intelligence. Our version of your CIA." He sat behind the desk again, folding his hands and letting them digest his words.

"Gregor Kulish was once a Colonel in the *Pogranichnyye Voiska*, the KGB arm responsible for border security. His many years in that post taught him all the ways people may be smuggled through different countries undetected. He now uses that knowledge to traffic in flesh, peddling those women and girls who are either desperate or stolen."

"Bull-fuckin'-shit," Horace said. "That's as wild a story as I've ever heard."

"That is because your world is rather small, I'm afraid," Boris said with no apparent rancor. "When the USSR dissolved, many former soldiers and spies were suddenly unemployed. Some, as does Kulish, now use their old skills in new ways."

"So why all the hiding?" Frank said. "Why not just put a bullet in his head next time you see him?"

"I wish it were so simple a thing, Mr. Powers. Firstly,

Kulish is never alone. He keeps several guards with him. Two of them I know were with him in the old days. Besides, he is only one man in a larger picture. The top man of those I pursue, to be sure, but cut the tallest tree and a dozen will grow from the stump. I must have as many of them as possible."

"Why tell us?" Frank asked. "We're not law enforcement or government. Why not go to them?"

"Kulish has eyes and ears in many places," Boris said. "At the moment, I know where he is, in a general way. I do not wish him to leave Atlanta before I can move." He sat again, spreading his hands.

"I wish your help, Mr. Powers," he said. "You are resourceful, courageous, loyal to your friends. And to certain ideals. You can go places and do things the authorities cannot. That I cannot as well, given my position."

"What is it you think I can do?" Frank asked. "LaRouche is obviously annoyed with me, or else why grab my friend? I can't exactly walk in and pretend nothing happened."

"To be sure," Boris said. "Yet does that not give you the perfect excuse to begin culling his herd?"

Frank winced. "I'm no executioner. I'm just a shylock trying to earn a living."

Boris leaned forward again, looking from one face to the next, his gaze drilling into theirs. "These men are evil, as Yvonne says. They will continue using and discarding little girls. They will continue turning people into slaves of whatever drugs they can sell. Are you not a man of ideals? Do you wish to see the weak of your city turned into livestock for Kulish's slaughterhouse?"

"And you," he said, turning to Yvonne. "Do you not bear some responsibility for those young ladies you lured to

LaRouche's stable? For make no mistake, those not already broken to his saddle will soon be so."

Yvonne turned away, cheeks flushed. "I didn't know—"

"No you did not," Boris said, not unkindly. "Yet now you do."

"That all don't mean shit to me," Horace began, but Boris cut him off, one hand chopping the air.

"Mr. Greene, do you have any idea at all how the Russians view your kind? I do not care who you find attractive, but many of Kulish's people would be happy to carve you and anyone with you into dog meat. If they are able to secure a strong enough control in this city, they will do just that. Not for any business reasons, simply for their own entertainment."

Horace didn't blush like Yvonne. His face turned empty and cold. Frank knew he was remembering the old days, the rednecks and hicks of his hometown.

"So," Boris said, settling back. "You help me, and I help you, yes?"

"What do we need help with?" Frank asked.

"Quite a lot, I think," Boris said. "There is the small matter of the phone call one of your clients—a Mr. Bradshaw, I believe—made to the local FBI about an extortionist threatening him with blackmail and poison."

"That little pig-fucker!" Horace said, standing up. "Boss, I told you not—"

"And Madame LaRouche," Boris said, interrupting. "She is known to the authorities as a person of interest, although they do not have enough to arrest her. Yet."

"You wouldn't," Yvonne said, although she had gone from pink to pale.

"No, indeed," Boris said. "*I* would not. Do you not think

your so-called husband would sell you in minutes to save his own skin? I have friends in various American agencies who will ensure you are forgotten. If you help me with Kulish."

The room fell silent, four sets of eyes shifting from one face to another.

"Well, hell," Horace finally said. "I got no use for people who don't like me, sure enough. And I never did much care for Rooskies."

"I guess you have Yvonne and me by the short hairs," Frank said. "And you're right. I don't like what's been done. Yvonne?" Frank turned to her, eyebrows raised.

"Dammit," she said, exhaling a long gust too forceful to be a sigh. "I'm pissed about Savannah and Sunset. I'm in."

"Excellent," Boris said. "Now, what do you need from me?"

"How about a few more warm bodies..." Frank began, stopping when Boris shook his head.

"I am truly sorry," Boris said. "I and my men must remain unknown for now. All I can say is we will not help LaRouche's or Kulish's men in any confrontation with you."

"Okay," Frank said. "I guess it's just the three of us then."

"Fantastic," Horace said with a wry snort.

CHAPTER 14

THE STARS TWINKLED AND MOONBEAMS KISSED THE landscape as Frank drove back toward North Druid Hills and his tiny, battered, threadbare office. He couldn't wait to get there, to where things were familiar and made sense.

Yvonne sat beside him, quiet and thoughtful, staring ahead without really seeing the road. Horace sat in the rear, leaned up against the door with his legs stretched across the seat. He wasn't saying much either.

As for Frank himself, he wished he could start a conversation. About the weather, the abysmal year the Braves were having, the price of sushi...anything to shut his own whirling thoughts down, at least for a little while.

The only sounds were tires on the road, cars passing by, the air-conditioned breeze.

The truth was, Frank hadn't been a leg-breaker for over ten years. He'd gone into loansharking because it paid better and the pigeons were less likely to peck. With the "agonist" schtick, they never did. Frank let them see whatever threats their own minds came up with, which was much easier.

Frank was a fairly lazy guy at heart.

Then again, LaRouche had grabbed Horace and beat the shit out of him. Maybe not put him in the hospital, but Ace would be carrying some impressive bruises for a couple of weeks. That deserved something.

He still wasn't sure why Yvonne was so important to LaRouche. He knew some guys couldn't stand the thought of their women running off, but LaRouche was in the women business. Surely he could replace Yvonne without much trouble. Unless she really was that indispensable to his business operation. In which case she was probably holding something back from Frank. Not to cause trouble, maybe. Something in reserve in case she needed a little extra persuasiveness.

All these thoughts ran circles in his head, like a mouse in a metal wheel. Round and round, going nowhere as he parked the Audi in front of the office door.

The parking lot was usually empty this late in the evening. The dentist's office was deserted, and Larry the Lawyer rarely worked late.

So why was a panel van parked a few spaces away?

The van had a logo painted on its flat, white side: *Liebowitz Exterminators - We Pester Your Pests*. A little cheesy, and a little ominous.

Horace leaned forward, his head between Frank's and Yvonne's.

"Light under the door, Boss."

"Shit," Frank said, then heaved a sigh. Part of him was annoyed, but a different part, a far larger part, was happy. At least this was something he could deal with here and now. Something straightforward and simple.

"Guns?" Yvonne asked.

"Not here," Frank said. "The road's too close. Too much chance of someone hearing. I figure whoever's in there is thinking the same."

He watched the narrow crack under the door. The light shone steady, unbroken. No one stood between the overhead bulbs and the door. No ambush seemed likely. Probably the nimrods inside planned to bluster and pose before giving them all a good beating.

Frank smiled. Yvonne had that flush in her cheeks again. Horace grinned like a cat. This should help relieve the tension. Not to mention limbering them up for what might be coming. They might get some information, of course, but that was secondary at best.

They left the machine pistols in the trunk.

Frank studied the door, noticed the bent frame beside the lock plate. Crowbar, probably. At least he wouldn't have to replace the knob and deadbolt, but setting a new frame would be a pain. Ah, well.

Frank pushed the door inward, stepping back a couple of paces so his face was out of the direct glow of fluorescent light, Yvonne and Horace right behind and on either side.

Only two goons waited inside. About six hundred pounds between them, but still only two. One sat on the edge of the desk, watching the door. The other was pawing through the desk, scattering papers and office supplies all over the floor. Had to be LaRouche's. Big, wide, dark hair, black suits.

Both goons looked up when he opened the door.

"You Powers?" asked the one sitting on the desk.

"Yeah, me Powers. And you trespassing. Get the hell out of my office."

"Oh, we will," said the one going through the drawers. "In just a few minutes. 'Course, you'll be coming along."

"With the two of you?" Frank asked. "When's your boss going to learn? Two of his twerps aren't enough to even be annoying."

"Y'all are makin' a hell of a mess," Horace said. He walked past Frank, knelt down, and began scooping the scattered files into a pile.

"You must be Powers' faggot friend," Goon Number One said. "I think we're safe leaving you here." He raised his foot, meaning to kick or push Horace away.

Horace dropped the papers, grabbed the foot, yanked it.

As the startled goon slid off the desk toward him, Horace punched him squarely in the crotch, a straight jab with his entire shoulder behind it.

The face above the black suit went dead white. His mouth opened, but all that came out was a breathy mewling, which cut off as Horace punched him again. He fell in a heap, a dark stain spreading in the front of his pants.

At least this one wouldn't be raping any hookers for a while.

The second goon gawped for a second, but recovered quickly. One hand dipped into his jacket pocket and came out with something black and stubby. He swung it up toward Horace.

Frank hurled himself forward, striking Horace as the goon pulled the trigger.

With a low pop of compressed gas and the crackle of electricity, taser darts flew, and bit into Frank's chest.

Frank gave a strangled grunt as his muscles locked in a single massive, agonizing cramp. He fell backward, trailing the fine coppery wires and twitching. Wide awake but unable to move. He felt like hornets were stinging his entire body.

He saw Horace jump onto the desk and kick the bastard under the chin. Hard, but not hard enough to break his jaw. Good. Frank needed the guy to talk. At least he would, as soon as he could talk himself. The goon's head snapped back, bounced off the wall, and he went down in a heap.

Yvonne yanked the barbs out of Frank, then made sure the first guy was still down.

"You want this one too?" she asked.

"Maybe later," Frank said, teeth chattering. "Don't axe him yet, but make sure he stays, quiet, won't you?"

Yvonne smiled sweetly, then swung her right leg in a tight roundhouse kick, driving the hard toe of her boot into the prone man's temple. He jerked once, then his eyes rolled up and he went still.

Frank's muscles vibrated and he felt weak, but he'd live. He tore off a piece of his shirt and pressed it to the two small punctures.

"How you feeling, Boss?" Horace asked.

"I'll be sore tomorrow, but I'm okay."

Frank sat up, rubbing the back of his neck. He pointed to the white-eyed form lying on the carpet. "Check that one out, Ace."

"Aw shit, girl," Horace said, eying the unconscious man. "Did you kill him?"

"Don't worry," she said, helping Frank to his feet. "He'll wake up. Eventually. With one hell of a headache."

Frank opened the bottom right-hand desk drawer, pulled out a large roll of heavy black duct tape, and tossed it to Horace.

"Get his hands and ankles?" he said. "And make sure he stays quiet until we need to talk to him."

"You got it, Boss," Horace said, pulling a length of tape with a loud purr. "How 'bout his buddy?"

Yvonne helped Frank lift the second goon into a chair, then the two of them taped his legs and forearms to the heavy wood. They used the last of the roll to wind his chest a few times.

Yvonne filled a cup with ice water from the cooler and dumped it down the front of the man's shirt.

He gasped and spasmed, held by the loops of tape, and opened his eyes. He didn't take long to grasp the recent change in his status.

The goon worked his jaw from side to side and glared at Frank, Yvonne, and Horace in turn. An impressive welt under his chin promised to bloom into a truly magnificent bruise.

"Now then," Frank said. "Mind telling me why you damaged my door and violated my personal space?"

"I don't gotta tell you shit," the goon said, sneering up at them.

The sneer vanished and his eyes went wide as Yvonne took a pen from the desk and slid it into his left ear.

"Be nice now," she said, kissing his cheek as she poked around in his ear.

"Yvie," Frank said, his hand on her shoulder. "I need him to be able to hear me."

Yvonne pouted cutely, but took the pen away. She didn't put it down, however. She sat where the goon could see her and twiddled it in her fingers. When his stare flicked from the pen to her eyes, she winked.

"Okay, Sparky," Frank said, grabbing his chin, fingering

the knot. The way the bound man's eyes watered was oddly satisfying. "Why don't you tell me your name?"

"Fuck you," he said, and tried to spit. Nothing came out. Frank imagined his mouth was pretty dry, given the circumstances.

Frank drove the heel of his hand into the goon's forehead, rocking his head back, wrenching his neck.

"How about you drop the tough guy bullshit and answer my questions?"

The goon shook his head, not in denial but trying to clear it. That kind of shot usually left a person pretty loopy, and his neck muscles would be sore as hell tomorrow.

"Name?" Frank asked again. He kept his voice light, conversational. Businesslike.

"Silcox," he finally said. "Jack."

"That's better," Frank said, smiling and leaning back. "Okay, Jack. Why did you come here?"

"The big man told us to wait here in case you showed up," Silcox said. "What did you think?"

Yvonne brought the tip of the pen toward his right eye.

"Be nice," she said. "Or I won't be."

"Yvie," Frank said, waggling a finger at her. She blew him a kiss, then moved to Silcox's lap, pen held ready. What a woman!

"What were you supposed to do when we showed up?" Frank asked.

Silcox was now in the confusing position of having a sexy bombshell on his lap, threatening to blind him with a Bic pen. Frank could see his brain starting to short out.

"Where else did the 'big man' send people?" Frank asked.

"I dunno," Silcox said. "Your place. Greene's. I don't know where else."

"And what were you planning to do when we showed up?"

Yvie doodled on his nose, the ink smearing as Silcox began to sweat.

"We were supposed to bag you," Silcox said. "Take you to the Boss. I don't know why."

"Where would that be?" Frank asked.

"His club. The one on Cheshire Bridge. The White Russian."

"It's called The White Russian?" Horace said. "Please tell me you're kidding."

"Well," Frank said, looking around at his partners. "Who am I to refuse an invite? Let's truss these guys and leave 'em in back."

The last thing Silcox saw was Frank's elbow speeding toward his temple.

CHAPTER 15

As the three drove through the humid blanket of an Atlanta summer night toward the fleshpots of Cheshire Bridge Road, Frank was thinking hard.

What the hell had he gotten into here? In less than forty-eight hours, he'd gone from a simple guy with a simple life to tearing all over one of the biggest cities in the country, wrapped up in some international slave ring, with a woman who'd turned his life inside out a couple of times already. Now she was doing it again.

Still, he had to admit that part of him enjoyed this. An older part, the one that used to hurt people for fun and profit. The danger was exciting. Different from leaning on small-time pimps, bar owners, or yuppies living beyond their means.

Time to fess up, at least to himself. He was having fun. And having Yvonne back in his life and bed was most definitely a plus.

It wouldn't last. It never had. She was far too independent to stay with him for long.

So why had she gotten married?

Good question.

Frank glanced at Yvonne, then back to the road.

"I think it's time we talk," he said, giving her hand a squeeze. "What's the deal with you and LaRouche? Why'd you marry him? I thought you weren't the marrying kind. Or even the long-term relationship kind."

Yvonne sighed, squeezing his hand in return. "I wanted... I don't know. I thought some stability would be nice. And he *is* rich. It was mostly a business decision. No heavy emotion to get in the way."

Horace snorted from the back seat. Frank and Yvonne ignored him.

"Did you know about Kulish?" Frank asked.

"I knew a little," Yvonne said. "He's very suave. Very polished. You'd think he's an old country gentleman." She shuddered. "I knew they were up to something. Lots of late-night phone calls, which isn't unusual in our business, but very hushed voices. And then..."

"Then what?" Horace asked. He was leaning forward now. Frank knew Ace. He was getting caught up in spite of himself.

"Then girls started disappearing," she said in a low voice. "And started showing up again. Hurt, hooked, sometimes dead."

Frank heard something in her voice that he didn't recognize. He looked over and was surprised, and moved. She wiped at her eyes, her usual tough manner laid aside.

"That's why I had to leave," she said after a bit. "Immoral vice is one thing." She gave a shaky little laugh. "But I couldn't be part of this. People are free to choose their own road to pleasure or pain. When it's their own choice. No one should be forced. No one should be a slave."

Frank put his arm around her shoulder. She laid her cheek on his hand for a moment, then lifted it away, kissing it gently.

"I'm no saint," she said. "But I never hurt kids if I can help it. That's all these girls are, you know. Most of them can't buy their own beer yet."

She looked over at Frank, then back at Horace. Frank saw glistening droplets in her lashes and felt his heart thaw a little more.

"I hate that bastard," she whispered. "Him and that rotten fuck Kulish. I'd like to kill them myself, but I'd rather stake them out and bring all the people they've hurt to pay them back."

"Shit," said Horace. His own voice low. "Gal's got a heart after all."

Her shoulders jerked.

"Hey, sorry honey," Horace said, patting her shoulder. "I'm no good at this emotional stuff. I'll help you, though. I been beat up, spat on, and treated like shit for way too much of my life. I know what it's like when you ain't got a whole lot and people take even that much away. That girl y'all found with me didn't need any of what she got from them boys. Maybe that don't mean much from the likes of me, but..."

"Thank you, Horace," Yvonne said, and put her soft, delicate hand over his gnarled, knuckly one. "It means a lot. Love you, honey."

Frank couldn't believe his ears. Well, he told himself that. The truth was, he knew Horace and Yvonne like he knew himself.

They all came from less than idyllic backgrounds and made their way through life as best they could. Using other people, taking advantage sometimes, but always deeply loyal to their friends.

That's how life was for their kind. True families got forged from mutual love and respect among the world's underbelly. Families stronger than accidents of biology.

"How 'bout you, Boss?" Horace asked, clapping Frank on the shoulder. "You been awful quiet. That sure ain't like you."

"You know me, Ace," Frank said. His own throat felt a little tight. "I'm all about civic duty and compassion. I'll see it through, and not just because of Yvonne's borscht buddy."

Yvonne punched his shoulder and Horace snorted, which lightened Frank's mood.

"Let's go play hero," he said. "If any of us remember how."

CHAPTER 16

The parking lot of The White Russian was packed. Typical for a Thursday night. Frank had never really understood why Thursday was the big party night in Atlanta, but what the hell. A lot of things about this city didn't make much sense.

They drove slowly across the cracked asphalt, to the very back of the lot. Behind them, they could hear the muffled thump-thump-thump of dance music from the club. Only a few sodium arc lights fought against the darkness of the lot. The club itself was blacked out, except for lights over the main entrance and a small service door at the rear. No neon, no flash. On the outside, at least.

Across a narrow strip full of sickly grass and weeds sat a squat cinderblock building, looking abandoned.

"There," Yvonne said. "Let's start there."

"Why the hell you want to go in there?" Horace asked.

She turned to him and gave a grim, tight smile.

"It's Quentin's warehouse."

Frank killed the lights and the engine. They got out, not

worrying about noise. Between the club and Atlanta's general roar, no one inside would hear them.

Frank shed his jacket and left it in the back seat. He opened the trunk, handing Horace one of the machine pistols they'd liberated from his captors, and took the other for himself.

Yvonne took the sheathed knife from her boot and tucked it into her waistband, leaving her hands free.

"This way," she said in a low voice.

She led them past the front door, around the corner, and to a dusty, unused loading dock.

Frank realized he was supposed to *think* it unused. The dust on the ramp had been swept in from the sides, not quite filling in the tracks of many vehicles. The detritus on the dock itself—paper, cans and bottles, a couple of girly magazines—was too clean. Wet from the earlier storm, but not covered with grime like it should be. Camouflage.

They followed Yvonne, creeping up the steps to the smaller doorway beside the large loading gate. She tried the knob. Locked.

Frank borrowed Yvonne's knife, prying the wood trim apart until there was a gap by the knob he could slip the blade through. He jiggled the knife this way and that, and was rewarded by the feel of the latch popping back. Commercial knobs were trickier than domestic, but he'd had a lot of practice over the years. He pushed the door open an inch at a time, carefully and slowly.

No light came around the door. Frank opened it all the way and they stepped quickly into the darkness. The smell of damp cardboard and rodent shit assaulted his nose, and he had to pinch his nostrils until the urgent need to sneeze passed.

There was another odor as well, a thin coppery smell he recognized. Not fresh, thank goodness.

Someone or many someones had shed blood in here, but not recently.

Frank and Yvonne pulled their cell phones out, the dim light enough to save their toes without alerting any of the occupants. He hoped.

When Frank shut the door, the normal Atlanta traffic noise, on the roads and in the air, vanished like he'd thrown a switch. He shone his feeble light in a wide arc. He saw stacked piles of crushed boxes, a tangle of bent and broken chairs, and a heap of mildewed garments. Women's clothes, from the look.

The walls a double course of ten-inch block, the door itself thick and backed with studio baffling. The whole building was soundproofed.

He was afraid he knew why.

Yvonne leaned in, pulling Frank and Horace close. "Downstairs," she whispered.

The three went through the loading area, down a short hallway, and finally to an elevator and stairwell. Through the gloomy light from the parking lot, Frank could see a shabby looking lobby space, without furniture and scattered with dust bunnies. Whatever this building had once been, no one had come through the front door in a long, long time.

They crept down the stairs, Frank in the lead. Yvonne was right behind him, and Horace brought up the rear. They moved slowly, placing their feet instead of stepping, making no noise.

They heard noise, though. Muffled sobbing, from more

than one source. Something that sounded like a prayer, but in a language Frank didn't know. Slavic, maybe.

At the bottom of the stairs was a tiny landing, only as wide as the steel-banded door ahead. There was no window, but it was slightly ajar and a dim band of light showed around the edges.

Frank bent close, listening. Nothing but assorted sounds of miserable women.

No sense being coy. He shoved the door open and the three of them burst into the room, guns and knife raised.

No one there. Just a long corridor, as wide as the stairwell and elevator, thick doors lining the walls. Some barred on the outside, some not. A row of twin-bulb fluorescents split the ceiling, most of the tubes guttering and weak.

They walked down the hall, wary as cats. until—

Behind them, Frank heard the unmistakable, testicle-tightening sound of more than one shotgun shell jacking home.

Shit.

CHAPTER 17

"You must be Powers," said one of the unseen gunmen. "How about you and your buddy lay those grease guns down, nice and slow."

No help for it. Frank and Horace unslung the Steyrs and lowered them to the floor, then rose up again, hands out away from their sides.

"Smart man," the voice said. "See, Eugene? The boss said he's smart. Now, keep your hands away from your bodies, away from each other's bodies too, and turn around."

They did so, and got blinded when two of the ambush party lit them up with high power flashlights.

Not before Frank counted five of them. Not bruisers and not white trash. These guys looked competent. The two with the lights still held their shotguns pointed in Frank's direction. Casual but steady. Depending on the strength in their arms and the loads in the scatterguns, they might be able to shoot. Only once each, true, but once would be enough at this range. Shotguns weren't exactly precision instruments.

Between the two lights stood the other three. Frank's eyes started to adjust a little. All five of them were too relaxed, too calm. Totally in control. Pros.

A pity, that.

Yvonne pressed against Frank's back. She did her helpless damsel routine, which made anyone who knew her burst out laughing. She was good at it, though. She looked at their captors with wide eyes, her body shivered, she seemed on the verge of tears.

And she was pushing something down the rear of his pants, into his ass-crack. Something slim and hard, about four inches long, encased in what felt like leather.

Good girl!

The center guy, the one with the voice, pointed his shotgun at Yvonne's head.

"C'mon, girlie," he said, managing to sound both cutesy and sardonic. "Your hubby misses you and wants you home."

Frank felt her push the knife down as far as she could before she stepped out from behind him, acting shaky and scared to death.

"He won't hurt me, will he Jack?" she asked in a small, breathy voice.

So she knew at least the one.

"Oh, I'd say you deserve at least a good spanking," Jack said, shaking his head sadly. "Running away from home, leaving us all worried and shit."

"I couldn't help it!" Yvonne said, starting to blubber. Damn she was good. "Some of Kulish's people wanted... wanted to..." She put her hands to her face and sobbed loudly.

"Can it, sister," Jack said. "You didn't want to help the

boss and you split. End of story. Get your ass over here and quit playing the fool, and I might—*might*—take you straight to him without letting the guys here start the spanking early."

What an asshole.

Yvonne threw her arms around Frank's neck, kissing his cheek then hugging him tight.

"Wait a while," she whispered in his ear, barely audible. "Give me tonight to work on Quentin, find out what I can, before you come."

She was one hell of a woman, no doubt about it. Here they were, facing a half-dozen jerks with shotguns, and the feel of her lips against his ear made him...

Sheesh!

He squeezed her back, hard enough that her spine crackled, then let her go.

Yvonne walked over to the one called Jack, shuffling along with her head down and shoulders slumped. Jack grabbed her arm and started marching her roughly back toward the stairs.

"Tie these assholes up," he said over his shoulder. "Then leave 'em down here and head back to the house. Eugene, you stay behind and keep an eye on them."

Eugene stood with his shotgun, a nice Browning pump-action ten gauge with a pistol grip and sawed-off barrel, pointed right at them. The short pipe and close quarters meant any shot would take out at least one of his buddies along with Frank or Horace. That didn't seem to bother the little twerp.

Unless it was loaded with slugs, of course.

They herded Frank and Horace into the room where Jack and his crew had been hiding. Several heavy wooden captain-style chairs sat around a small table. The dark oaken arms and spindles looked far too heavy for even Frank to break.

That was okay.

Horace and Frank were shoved back into the chairs, struggling against the three goons until Eugene jacked the shotgun again, pointing the barrel toward Horace's head this time.

That's the thing about shotguns, you don't aim them. You just point them in someone's general direction. With a sawed-off, you count on the pellet spread to hit anything at all, and they're useless past about ten yards. Up close, they're next to useless, unless the victim is standing right in front of the barrel.

Frank counted on Eugene's shotgun now, both its strengths and weaknesses.

Once he and Horace were trussed up, wrists and ankles tied to the chair arms and legs, Eugene took a seat and laid the Browning across his lap. The other three left without a word, the last closing the door behind him, cutting off the sniffles and sobs from the other rooms.

"So now what?" Frank asked Eugene.

"I don't know and I don't really care," their captor said.

"C'mon man," Horace said. "Give us a clue, why don't ya? I gotta know if I need to change my supper plans."

"Shaddup," Eugene said. "I think you're going to find out sooner than you want. The boss is pretty pissed at you two."

"What about *his* boss?" Frank asked. "The Russian?"

"No idea," Eugene said. "But he's LaRouche's partner, not boss."

"That's not what Boris told me," Frank said. "He made it sound like LaRouche is Kulish's puppy dog."

"What the hell would that ape know?" Eugene said. "He's a dumb shit that barely speaks English." He didn't sound angry. Just bored. Guard duty was never all that exciting. If you were lucky.

Frank didn't plan on him being lucky for long.

With no warning, Frank began to thrash his body side to side, pulling against the bonds on his legs and wrists. He grunted with effort, his face flushing.

Eugene got up, cradling his gun, not in any hurry. He strolled to where Frank whipped back and forth like a fish on a hook, and lightly bonked him on the top of the head with the shotgun's barrel.

"Stop it, genius," he said. "You're big, but you're not going to break two-inch-thick red oak. Just relax before you strain something." He went back to his own chair, sat down, and rocked it back against the wall.

Frank subsided. He knew he couldn't break the wood. That wasn't the point at all. He figured ol' Eugene had never been tied to a chair before.

He panted for a couple of minutes, then yawned. And yawned again.

Then Horace yawned.

And then Eugene yawned, right on cue.

They sat together in silence for about an hour, Frank nodding and jerking back up from time to time. He let his head droop again, slowing his breathing, relaxing.

Beside him, Horace slumped. He started snoring. Just a little, like any old fart taking a nap.

Frank breathed slowly and deeply, listening. It didn't take long.

He heard Eugene yawn loudly. He heard him get up and walk toward them. He felt a hand checking the bindings on his wrists.

Then he heard the door open, and footsteps fading down the hall. Their guard was tired, bored, and needed to stretch his legs.

God bless human nature.

With a single violent surge, Frank heaved himself upright, the heavy wood separating at nearly every join.

No way to break the wood, true.

But glue? He could break glue.

He stood, still tied to the chair arms and legs, but more mobile than he had been. He bent over, tugging the knots at his ankles until his legs were free.

Horace hissed at Frank. "Get over here. Gimme your arms."

In less than thirty seconds, Frank dropped the last bits of wood and dug Yvonne's knife out of his ass. Twenty seconds after that, Horace stood beside him.

Just in time, too.

Frank heard a toilet flush, footsteps returning up the corridor. Horace dropped back in his chair. Frank laid the ropes over his wrists. It didn't look at all convincing, but Eugene would only get a brief glance.

He had the knife, but unless he got a perfect hit, it wouldn't be quick enough. Frank picked up the back of his broken chair instead and stood beside the door.

The knob turned and the door swung open. Eugene stepped in, shotgun hanging from one hand. He stumbled over the pile of disjointed chair bits.

"What the—"

Frank swung the chair's back in a tight arc, the stout oak

catching Eugene in the center of his forehead with a dull crunch instead of a solid thunk.

Bad news for Eugene.

He stood there, swaying, his body not realizing his brain no longer worked. Then his glazed eyes rolled back in his head. The shotgun hit the floor right before Eugene did. He went straight down, his joints and muscles detached from his brain.

Horace sprang up and toward Frank, grabbing the gun off the floor.

"Aw hell, boss," Horace said with a staggering lack of sympathy. "I think you mighta hit him a wee tad too hard."

On the floor, Eugene's breath rattled weakly, a low snore coming from the back of his flaccid throat. His forehead had a distinct flat spot where the chair caught him. The skin was split and bleeding, but Frank doubted the guy had time to develop a bruise.

"Tsk. A damn shame," Frank said. "At least we don't have to tie him up."

"Let's get the hell outta here," Horace said. "What do we do about these gals?"

They went down the hall, checking the occupants in each room. None of them looked fit to travel. They didn't seem unhealthy, except for various welts and bruises, but all were clearly on something or other. Probably tranqs or Xanax.

"I hate to," Frank said, "but we need to leave them for now. We'll have to stow Eugene somewhere, though. And the busted chair. Leave 'em guessing if anyone comes around."

Horace sighed. "Always with you it's work, work, work."

CHAPTER 18

THEY DRAGGED EUGENE'S INERT BODY UP THE STAIRS TO THE empty loading room. Enough junk lay around to cover him up pretty well. Fortunately, the bleeding had stopped when his breathing did.

"Why the hell can't folks take a shit *before* they get kilt?" Horace said, pulling a face.

"It's all just to spite you, Ace," Frank said. "Here, help me see what all he's got."

In the dead man's jacket they found ten more shells for the Browning. Number ten birdshot. He was an inside man, then. Not out. Buckshot or slugs would blow right through a wall or a body at close range. Birdshot would make a hell of a mess, but without any penetration.

Frank let Horace keep the shotgun. Their Steyrs had gone with Jack's other help, so they had one gun, one knife, and no idea where they were going. At least they still had the car.

"We need to make a couple of stops, Ace," Frank said. He tossed the key to Horace. "You drive."

They needed some help, too. Time to make some calls.

Frank had Eugene's cell phone. He pulled it out and punched in directory assistance.

"City and state, please?" a pleasant southern matron asked.

"Atlanta, Georgia," Frank replied. "Number for Diamond Dogz nightclub."

"That's with a 'z', right sugar?" the operator said. "The number is 404-632-9250. I'll connect you now. Have a good night, sug."

"Thank you," Frank said, and waited while a rapid series of beeps beeped in his ear.

The call was answered after the first ring. A blare of music and shouts made Frank wince and pull the phone away.

"DDs," a man's voice yelled over the noise. "What can I do ya for?"

"This is Officer Gregory Yurin, Atlanta P.D." Frank said. "I need to speak with your head of security, a man named Boris I think, about a complaint registered by a patron."

"Oh fer Christ's sake," the man shouted, sounding disgusted. "Peabody's bitching again? Look, you tell that fat old bastard that no touching means—"

"Just let me speak to Mr. Boris, please," Frank said, trying to sound officious and annoyed. "This guy's a real tool, but we have to follow procedure."

A theatrical sigh came through. "Hang on."

He heard a click, a few seconds of a horrid Muzak version of *Sincerely*, then the familiar liquid accent.

"Mr. Powers, I believe?" Boris asked. "I must say, your make-believe name was very good. You are no Cosmonaut, but I don't think the great Yuri Gagarin would mind."

"I thought you'd like that," Frank said. "Listen, we were

just at LaRouche's storehouse beside The White Russian. We got jumped by a squad of his apes. They got Yvonne."

A brief pause then, "A shame," Boris said. "I am quite fond of that young lady, despite her many flaws."

"I'm pretty keen on her too," Frank said. "I'm going to go get her. And LaRouche."

"You must be careful, my friend," Boris said. "I'm sure he will be expecting you."

"I'm sure he will. That's why I'm calling. I need another man or two."

"I cannot. I have told you this already."

"Dammit, you listen to me!" Frank wasn't in the mood at all. "Don't be an asshole! They have the woman I...someone very important to me, and I mean to get her back. You said you want to stop LaRouche and Kulish, so act like it!"

There was silence for a minute. Frank would have thought Boris hung up, except he could still hear faint music from the club.

"I am an asshole, of course," Boris said. "As are we all, to a certain degree. But as I say, I am fond of Miss Yvonne. I can give you one man only. He is new, and therefore unknown."

"That should be enough," Frank said. "Is he good at quiet work? Blade or hands?"

"He is excellent at urban infiltration," Boris said. "He will be seen and heard only by those he chooses. He is also quite the expert with electronic devices, among other useful things."

"Good enough," Frank said. "Have him meet us in Decatur. 207 East Lake Drive. We'll be there in forty-five minutes." The townhouse Yvonne had taken him to should still be safer than his or Horace's place. He ended the call.

"Let's go. You still have your competition knives, Ace?"

"Yeah, at my place," Horace said, grinning. "Ain't had much chance to play with 'em in a while, but I'm still pretty good. I need some clean clothes anyhow."

"Good," Frank said. "Let's go get them. But first, stop by a convenience store. We need a few packs of chaw."

CHAPTER 19

HALF AN HOUR LATER, JUST PAST TWO O'CLOCK, FRANK parked the rented Audi in front of the townhouse.

He picked the lock easily, after first making sure no busybodies peeked out their windows, and went in. Horace followed him, shutting the door but not locking it.

Horace laid what looked like a chef's knife roll on the counter. They'd swung by his cozy little bungalow, only a few blocks from the office, to get his favorite toys. He'd also exchanged the green bandanna for red.

He'd unrolled the black canvas, revealing a beautiful set of five hand-forged spring steel throwing blades, when someone knocked softly on the door.

"Right on time," Frank said. He opened the door and a young man walked in, wearing black slacks, a black t-shirt, and the requisite shiny black leather jacket. A bright blue gym bag hung from his left hand.

"Boris has sent me to you," he said in a molasses-thick accent. "I am called Yakov Aronshtam."

"Jackoff?" Horace said, an overly innocent look on his face. "I never heard a name like that."

"No, please," he said patiently. "It is Yakov. I think you would say zhakob...yakob..."

"Jacob," Frank said. "Please to meet you, friend." He held out his hand, and Yakov shook. He was average-sized. Not nearly so tall and muscular as Boris or Frank himself. Not quite so wiry as Horace. Short blond hair was cut in that odd Slavic version of Parted Professional, the bangs a little long and swept to the side. He moved with a smooth confidence that reminded Frank of Yvonne. A trained fighter.

"And I you," Yakov said. "My commander tells me you will give help to him, to we, in destroying the *d'yavol* Kulish. You have the thanks of me and all those I know." He bowed over Frank's hand, embarrassing him a little.

"Hey now," he said, taking Yakov by the shoulders and pulling him upright. "We're all in this for our own reasons, but I admit I don't like this Kulish character, from what I've heard."

"We gotta wait on him, Jackoff," Horace said. "First we take down LaRouche and get the boss's girlfriend back."

"Jesus, Ace," Frank said. "Lay off with the assholese, would you?"

"Dang, dude," Horace said, trying to look hurt. "I'm only jokin' with him."

"I do not understand the joke," Yakov said.

"Never mind, big boy," Horace said. "You'll understand this."

He slid one of the knives from its pouch by the black, cord-wrapped handle. He balanced it for a moment before sending across the room with a quick flick of the wrist. Frank only saw a blur of silvery steel before the blade punched into the living room wall, almost twenty feet from where they stood.

"Very good," Yakov said, raising an eyebrow. "Few today practice the old skills." He dropped his bag and took a second knife from Horace's cloth, testing it just as he had. Holding it point down, arm dangling loosely, he suddenly flipped the blade underhand, sending it to strike the wall less than half an inch from the first.

"Not bad," Horace said, sauntering over to yank the knives free. It took some effort.

He went back the counter, took a wide fabric scabbard from the pouch and attached it to rear of his belt. The five blades went into the scabbard, and Horace's shirt fell over the handles.

"Did you bring any weapons?" Frank asked Yakov. "We aren't exactly overflowing with hardware."

"Of course," Yakov said, unzipping the bag. He took out two odd tools. They had wide, heavy, triangular blades, attached at right angles to short, bamboo handles. They looked like over-sized garden trowels that someone had gotten mad at.

"What the heck are those?" Horace asked.

"These are from Japan," Yakov said. "However, I obtained them here. They are rice farm *motygi*. I do not know the English...for cleaning around the food plants."

"Hoe. For digging weeds. Look sort of nasty," Frank said. He'd always had a healthy respect for lawn care imple-ments. "Why those?"

"I am a foreigner here," Yakov said, shrugging again. "But even in Ukraine, the garden shops do not ask questions."

Good point.

"How 'bout you, Boss?" Horace asked, taking a beer from the fridge and plopping down on a barstool. "Yvonne's pig-sticker enough for you?"

"You know me, Ace," Frank said, pulling a large saucepan down from the hanging pot rack. "I'm more dainty than you and Yvie. I'll stick with my little needle."

He emptied several pouches of shag chewing tobacco they'd bought down the street into the pot and added several inches of water from the kitchen tap. The pot and its foul contents went on the stove, and he lit the gas eye.

"We should probably go in the other room and shut the door," Frank said. "This place is going to smell like a spittoon for a while."

Sure enough, the kitchen began to reek like a honky-tonk's sidewalk a few minutes after the mess started to boil. Frank went back to the car to retrieve his jacket, then the three of them holed up in the largest of the place's three bedrooms, shutting the door and stuffing a bathroom towel against the crack along the floor.

"It is the concentrated nicotine, yes?" Yakov asked. Frank nodded, wiping his watering eyes.

"How long since you brewed that shit?" Horace asked. "I ain't heard of anyone you had to take out for a long while."

"Yeah, been a few years," Frank said. "Old skills die harder than old habits, I guess."

He and Horace had done all sorts of less-than-holy things back when they worked for hire. Assassination, for instance. Frank left civilians alone, as a rule. Unless they came to him for a loan. But the underworld types were almost always at odds among themselves. Sometimes secretly at odds with those who thought them bosom buddies.

Nasty, but folks choose the lives they lead, along with the consequences.

Frank and Horace both excelled at quiet death, though few who knew them these days realized it. Horace had his knives, Frank had his antique brass syringe.

It still had its uses in his new life, of course. The polished brass and wicked needle put the fright to people even before he started his bullshit "agonist" spiel. But it had other, far more genuine, uses.

They sat around for a while, talking weapons, tactics, and old lives. At least Frank and Horace talked old lives. This was Yakov's current life.

A couple of hours later, Frank went back to the kitchen, holding a wadded t-shirt from the bedroom's wardrobe over mouth and nose. He turned off the gas, and turned on every fan he could find. Horace came behind him, the red bandana now wrapped around his face instead of his hat, opening all the doors and windows.

Frank strained wads of brown glop from the pot, leaving a thickish, yellow syrup. He thinned it with a little water. Not much, just enough so that it could flow easily.

Horace found a funnel, drained the water from a plastic bottle with a French name on the label, and helped Frank pour the foul liquid from the pot.

It filled about two-thirds of the bottle. About fifteen ounces, Frank guesstimated. Should be plenty.

"Let's grab some shuteye," Frank said to his two companions. "Tomorrow's going to be a busy day, I think."

"You go on ahead, Boss," Horace said. "I reckon I'll stay up a bit and do a little practicin'. Been a while, and I need to knock the rust off."

"May I stay as well?" Yakov asked Horace. "Perhaps you

can show me this technique you use. Very different from me."

"You boys have fun," Frank said. "Try not to make too much noise." He walked back to the master bedroom, stripped down and slid between the sheets. Strange how quickly sleeping alone became odd. He knew Yvonne could take care of herself, so he told himself not to worry.

Frank drifted off to a land where a fiery redhead chose to share his life.

CHAPTER 20

Early the next day—early for folks in his profession anyway—Frank woke to the sound of a shower running. He yawned, swung his legs off the memory foam mattress, fighting to not lie right back down.

He stood, stretched toward the ceiling until a satisfying stream of crackles ran through his back and joints, then dressed and walked out to kitchen.

Horace was already awake, holding a huge mug of black coffee in both hands the way some people a religious talisman.

"Hey, buddy," Frank said, pouring his own cup of morning medicine. "How'd you sleep?"

"Like shit," Horace said, rolling his eyes. "Jackoff snores worse'n I do, and that's saying something."

"Poor guy," Frank said without sympathy. He'd shared sleeping quarters with his buzz-saw of a friend more than once. "I think you'll live."

Down the hall, the sound of running water died, and Yakov stepped into the hall, toweling his dripping hair. He wasn't wearing anything, and his lean body glistened under the fancy LED bulbs.

Frank looked him over. Not with lust. More the way he'd pick the right horse for a race. He didn't see any obvious weaknesses or flaws.

The Slav was compact. Muscular, without being huge. His skin as pale as only those of British or Scandinavian blood could manage, except where darker stripes and patches told of old wounds.

"Damn, son," Horace called. "Don't just stand there swingin' in the breeze. Get some clothes on!" In spite of his words, Frank noticed he didn't avert his eyes.

Yakov continued to rub his head. Frank could see patches of sneer through the cloth as he turned back to the smaller bedroom he'd slept in, muttering something in Ukrainian.

"Why are you giving him so much trouble, Ace?" Frank asked.

"I'm just messin' with him," Horace said, drinking his coffee. "He ain't half bad for an Ivan. We had a pretty good time talkin' last night."

"Oh yeah?" Frank said, eyebrows raised. "Talking, was it?"

Horace rolled his eyes. "Yessir, Mister Powers, sir. Just talking. What d'you take me for?"

"A lecherous old queer, eager to corrupt the youth," Frank said, grinning.

"Boss, it's too early for me to whup yer ass," Horace said with a grin of his own. "I'll give you a rain check, though."

"Fair enough," Frank said as Yakov came back in, tucking his shirt in his trousers.

"I am ready," he said. "Where do we first go?"

"That's a good question," Frank said. "I don't know where LaRouche's place is."

"Is on Paces Ferry Road," Yakov said. "One of the big bourgeois houses there, but he will not be home, I think."

"Why do you think so?" Frank asked, surprised. "And how do you know where he lives?"

"We keep very close watch on him," Yakov said with a shrug. "He has many of our young women held. He is also how we find Kulish. Kulish is very good at not being found."

"Where the hell's he at, then?" Horace asked. "If he ain't home, he's gotta be somewhere."

"Normally he spends his days at one or more of his clubs," Yakov said. "Trading either for weapons or flesh."

"He'll know we're coming," Frank said. "I'm sure some-one's noticed we aren't tied up in his jail anymore. So he probably won't be following his normal routine."

Yakov looked puzzled. "You were captured?"

"Yep," Horace said. "Trussed up like pigs. The guy with the shotgun wasn't easy to—"

Frank cut Horace off before he got on a roll. "A few of LaRouche's clowns bushwhacked us in the old office building he keeps the girls in," he said. "They only left one behind after they tied us down to a couple of old wooden chairs."

"The chairs came apart for you?" Yakov asked. Okay, this one *had* been tied to a chair before.

"Yeah," he said. "The watchdog went to take a leak, and caught a face full of wood when he came back."

"He is dead now?" Yakov asked. "That is both bad and good. He is one that our enemies cannot use, but now they must be alerted to you."

"The man's a damn genius," Horace said, shaking his head in mock wonderment.

"No, I am not," Yakov said gravely. "But I have been in this place before, both in the chair and guarding it."

"I was just..." Horace began. "Ah, hell. Forget it, Jack—Yakov. Let's go if we're going."

They gathered their various deadly weapons and headed out to begin the assault.

CHAPTER 21

FRANK DROVE WEST ALONG I-20, HEADING FOR THE northbound I-75. This close to noon, traffic was lighter than the usual four hour rush hour, but still heavy enough to require his full attention. Horace asked the questions now.

"So where we goin', Jack...Yakov?" he asked. "Paces Ferry's a purty long road."

"Not so far," Yakov said. "Maybe three kilometers from the highway. Then we must travel up King's Way."

"Not many houses back in there," Frank said, glancing at the Ukrainian in the rear-view mirror. "What's the best approach?"

"On foot, I think," Yakov replied. "Perhaps from a few hundred meters away. From the side, not front or back. This time of day, they must feel they can spot a man in the sunlight and so may not have so many watching away from the gates."

"You any good in the woods, boy?" Horace said, turning to look at Yakov. "That part of town's mostly trees, so the rich folks can pretend like they're all alone."

"I have much training in the forests between Ukraine and Slovakia," he said. "Much the same as the trees here. I will have no trouble."

"How about you, city boy?" Horace asked Frank.

"My dad and uncles used to drag me deer hunting," Frank said. "I might not be as good as you, country boy, but I should be okay. Especially since none of LaRouche's people we've seen so far look all that outdoorsy."

They merged onto West Paces Ferry Road, the Audi blending in with all the yuppie-mobiles. The only vehicle less conspicuous would have been a Hummer.

Buildings thinned as the exit-ramp strip malls gave way to McMansions, then the larger, older homes of Atlanta royalty gone by. Frank had worked with a few of them. Nice tippers and usually on time with payments. Threadbare or not, most of these places still had money floating around inside.

Five minutes later, they rolled past a grand old manor with high ivy-covered walls and a gate made of thick wrought iron. The way the black barricade glistened in the sunlight made it clear this was the real thing instead of a cheap modern substitute. Probably a hundred years old, and tough as only hand-worked metal can be. Frank figured the Audi might make it through, but wouldn't go very far after.

"Drive on, another kilometer maybe," Yakov said from the back seat.

Frank finally parked in a wooded area between two of the other estates. They got out and checked their gear. Frank tucked his handkerchief in the window facing the road, the universal sign of a breakdown. He didn't think there were any good Samaritans in the neighborhood, so there wouldn't be any cops or tow trucks. At least not for a few hours.

The trio took to the woods. Huge and ancient live oaks kept sightlines down to only a few yards, and regular rains kept the leaves and bracken moist enough that their feet made little noise.

Frank watched his companions with envy. Horace and Yakov flowed through the trees like wraiths. Frank did his best, but he was no real hunter. Every few minutes, either Horace or the Ukrainian hissed at him, frustrated with his lack of skill.

Finally, after skirting a couple of the massive privacy walls, they stopped a few hundred feet away from the wall marking the eastern edge of LaRouche's place. With all the oaks and what Horace called "yaller pine," the trees draped in purple-flowering wisteria and English ivy that had escaped from the manicured grounds all around, there was no danger of being spotted unless one of LaRouche's goons came through the woods.

Horace came close to Frank, speaking in low whisper. "Now what, Boss?"

Frank tapped Yakov's shoulder. "How about it?" he said, voice as low as Horace's. "What do you know about his setup?"

"Not so much," Yakov said. "Only Boris has been inside the walls. He says the man keeps maybe five guards. Armed, naturally."

"Probably shotguns again," Horace said. "Nothin' high-powered. Ain't no one gonna hear a shotgun with all the trees and bricks between houses."

"No way to see past the wall," Frank said. "No openings on this side."

"You really are a city boy, ain't you?" Horace said, grinning. He stripped off his shoes and socks, handed Frank his hat, and scrambled up into one of the bigger oaks, climbing like a monkey until Frank lost sight of him. Only a few shaking branches marked his progress.

Several minutes later, Frank nearly jumped out of his skin when Horace dropped from the tree right beside him. Little bastard.

"All right," he said. "I seen three of 'em from here. One dude at the front corner, mainly watching the gate. Two more walkin' around the house in opposite directions. Maybe four minutes when they're on the other side. I was right, Boss. All of 'em have shotguns just like Eugene's."

"Don't preen," Frank said, smiling at his fiend's smug expression. "It's ugly on you. Any sign of LaRouche?"

"Nope," Horace said. "But did you really expect the big dog would be out with the hired help?"

"Cameras?" Frank asked.

"Didn't see none," Horace said. "But I'm pretty sure the ol' boy's got some."

Frank checked his watch. "It's about twelve-thirty. Lunch time. I bet the guy on monitor duty isn't paying much attention right now."

"We cannot be so sure," Yakov said. "Now is best time, I agree. But we must move quickly to neutralize the three men outside and disappear into the house."

"You think he's in there, Boss?" Horace asked.

"I've got a feeling, yeah." Frank said. "I think he'll be doing what everyone does when they're trying to duck their responsibilities."

Of course, most of Frank's pigeons didn't have firepower and muscle on hand, but...

"So," Yakov said. "We must wait for the two walkers to be behind the house, then we must get over the wall and dispose of the stationary guard."

"Sure," Horace said, rolling his eyes. "We'll just float over the wall. I think I got some pixie dust—"

"Can it, Ace." Frank said. He looked around the woodlot until he found what they needed. A live oak with one massive limb only about a yard from the top of the wall.

"There," he said, pointing at the tree. "We'll use that. Ace, you're the smallest. Peek through the leaves. When the patrollers clear the corners, we'll all jump across."

"Um," Horace said, looking at him like Frank was nuts. "You do know there's broken glass all over the top of that thing, right?"

"So be careful," Frank said. "And fast."

"You get me into more crap..." Horace grumbled. He picked up his shoes, stuffing his socks inside. He tied the laces together and hung them around his neck, then was up the tree and scooting along the limb on his belly.

Frank and Yakov also removed shoes and socks, following Horace's example. Yakov went up the tree only a little slower than Horace.

Frank dragged himself after them as best he could. "Screw this shit," he said under his breath, trying not to pant any louder than he had to.

Soon they were lined up along the branch. Bless live oak, it didn't even tremble under their combined weight. Horace held his hand back, fingers open. One by one, he began to fold them down.

Three...two...one...

Horace came up on his hands and feet. He crept out as close to the wall as he could and jumped. Yakov followed, then Frank.

He wasn't a praying man normally, and regretted that a little as he made his leap.

Three feet to the wall, a foot across, and about eight feet down. Frank landed heavily on the soft lawn, going down to his knees with a low grunt.

Horace and Yakov were already on the move, running right up to the outside wall of dark aged brick, avoiding the four ground-floor windows. Frank got up, wincing as his right knee twinged, and followed.

By the time he got to the wall, Yakov had already grabbed the corner guard, hand around his mouth and nose, pulling him back. Horace drew one of his knives and skewered the hapless man's larynx, preventing any screams.

Yakov held him until he went limp, then laid him out. Horace had the guard's shotgun, another Browning 10, which he handed to Frank.

"You're better with these things than I am, Boss," he said, cleaning his blade on the dead man's jacket. "I'll stick to my stickers."

"You stay here," Frank said. He quickly checked the gun's chamber and thumbed the safety off, making sure it was ready to go. "Yakov, you take the back corner. I'll cover you both."

Horace crouched down below the level of the windows and moved to the front corner, a gleaming dagger in each hand. The blade in his right point-forward, the one in his left laid back along his forearm.

Frank glanced over to check on Yakov, but he was

already nearly invisible at the back corner, behind the leaves of a dense holly bush. Man must have some tough skin. Frank put his shoulders to the wall, shotgun held barrel up, ready to shoot to either side.

CHAPTER 22

FRANK HEARD A LOW SOUND OF FEET CRUNCHING IN GRAVEL from his right and crackling leaves from his left as the two guards strolled back around. The one behind the house was whistling. *Sweet Gypsy Rose,* of all things.

Horace's target came into view first.

He came straight up from his hunker, right hand driving in under his victim's sternum, left hand slashing across the throat. It was over in less than a second.

Blood sprayed from an open carotid and the man's shotgun dropped as his body sagged. Frank could see his mouth working uselessly. Scarlet runnels poured from his mouth and down his chin.

Horace caught the body and eased it to the ground.

From Yakov's corner, he heard the second guard break into a run as he called out.

"Hey, what the—"

A squelching *thunk* cut his yell short as Yakov swung one of the heavy Japanese hoes into his neck, right below the base of his skull.

The second guard fell, a puppet with cut strings. Yakov

had severed his spine, the wide trowel nearly decapitating the dead man.

"Well," Frank said. "That was quick."

He'd never felt so unneeded in his life, for which he was a little chagrined, and a little grateful.

They dragged the two corpses as close to the wall as possible, since Frank figured the cameras were wide-field and therefore blind this close to the house.

"Back door," he said, and three went behind the house to wait.

It didn't take long.

The door opened and a fourth flunky came out. A kid with longish, professionally messy hair. He was scrawny, pale, and unarmed, a geek if ever Frank had seen one. The kid carried a huge sandwich in his hands and sported a smear of mustard across one cheek. He looked about twenty. Maybe.

"Jesus, guys," he said around a mouthful of food. "I told ya, you gotta stay at least ten feet out from—"

Yakov and Horace grabbed his arms, and Frank jammed the shotgun's barrel hard up under his chin.

"Hi," Frank said. "Would you mind keeping your voice down, son?"

"S-s-sure..." he replied, the sandwich pulping between his trembling fingers. "W-who—"

"Shhh." Frank said. "You don't have any questions, but you might have answers. What's your name?"

"F-Fred."

Fred? Really?

Yakov yanked Fred's left arm around into a vicious hammerlock, pushing the wrist brutally up between his shoulderblades, then eased off just a bit. The sandwich hit the deck.

Yakov spoke quietly and calmly into his ear.

"Please, you will answer the questions, yes?"

The guard nodded rapidly, coughing as he tried to force his food down a no-doubt dry throat.

"Good boy, Freddie," Horace said, patting him on the head with his free hand.

"How many inside?" Frank asked.

"J-j-j-just t-two," he said. "And the m-m-maid." He was either a stutterer, or about to piss himself.

"LaRouche?"

Another jerky nod.

"Yvonne?"

"I don't—"

"Miss LaRouche, ya dummy," Horace said, shaking him like a terrier with a rat.

"No, she's gone. She went with the Russian."

Shit.

"Okay, son," Frank said. "Now you're going to take us in, tell us where the others are, then we're going to tie and gag you. Understand?"

"Please, mister," he said, starting to cry. "I'm just a techie. I just work the surveillance. Lemme go?"

"You keep bein' a good little puppy and we'll turn you loose," Horace said.

"We must restrain you until we finish with your employer," Yakov said.

"By the way, Fred," Frank said, his voice lowering as they all went inside. He switched the barrel from Fred's chin to the back of his head. "Where is the good lord of the manor?"

"In his study," Fred said.

"And the other guards?"

"I don't know for sure. Honest."

A kid named Fred who used words like honest. Frank felt like he was in a bad movie.

"Best guess?"

"Tim was in the kitchen, last I saw," Fred said. "We were having lunch. Walter's with Mr. LaRouche in his office."

"I am sorry for causing you to drop your lunch," Yakov said. "I will make you another before we leave."

Horace rolled his eyes. "Right little gentleman ain't you, Jackoff?"

"He helps us, we should be as polite as we may," Yakov replied. "This one is no hurter of women, I think."

The back door opened into a small foyer. What looked like closet doors flanked them. A hallway led straight in, more doors on either side. Two on the left, three on the right. Frank could hear a washing machine sloshing away behind the closest.

"Quiet down everyone," Frank said, then whispered to Fred. "Which way to the kitchen? And if I don't have to strain to hear the answer, my buddy here will stick a knife in your ear."

"First door on the right," Fred barely breathed.

Yakov released his hold on Fred, taking the lead.

They inched forward, making no noise except the occasional sniffle from their captive. Yakov put his ear to the door, listened a moment, and shook his head.

Frank and Horace moved in front of the door as Yakov stepped aside, pulling on a pair of supple leather gloves. Frank laid the shotgun on Fred's right shoulder.

Yakov gripped the handle, turned it, and flung the door

wide. Frank shoved Fred through then he, Yakov, and Horace swept in. Yakov closed the door silently.

They saw no one in the large, brightly-lit kitchen. Only a long work table with the plates and glasses for two meals. A white, four-panel door beside a gigantic stainless steel refrigerator stood slightly ajar, opening into the space beyond.

Frank relaxed a little, but came back to full attention when a toilet flushed behind it. Flushing toilets seemed an awfully important part of his life recently.

He moved to stand beside the door and brought the butt of the shotgun up, preferring blunt trauma to gunshots at the moment.

Horace laid a hand over Fred's mouth and a keen line of steel against his neck.

Yakov pushed the smaller man and his captive slightly, positioning them right across from the bathroom while sounds of hands being scrubbed came from the slightly cracked door, then came up beside Frank and got to the floor in front of it.

This should be interesting.

The door opened and another guy with salt and pepper hair, jutting cheekbones, and shoulders that strained his black suit came out.

The guard saw Horace holding Fred and started forward, not making a sound until he tripped over Yakov with a grunt. Frank helped him down to the floor with a full swing of the Browning, the heavy wooden stock like a sledgehammer. The goon cooperated by not moving again.

Fred's eyes were the size of dinner plates. He didn't try to get away, not that he'd be able to with Horace and his knife skills. He stood there, pressed back against the older man, stiff as a post. Frank barely heard his repeated whispers. "Ohgodohgodohgod…"

"Buck up, son," Horace said, his voice bright and cheery. "He ain't dead. Just sleepin'. Gonna have one hell of a noggin thumper when he comes to, though."

The rising odor of urine from the downed man marked Horace's dishonesty, but Fred didn't need to know.

"Come on guys," Frank said as Yakov rose, brushing his knees. "Hey, Fred. Where's the monitor room?" Jesus, he sounded like Barney Rubble.

"Across the hall," the kid said. He'd lost the stutter. His voice was flat and his face slack. If he wasn't in shock already, he'd at least gone down the exit ramp.

Frank went through the drawers until he found a cloth to carefully wipe down everything he touched.

Hell of a day to forget his gloves.

Yakov cracked the kitchen door to take a peek down the hall. He flashed a circle of finger and thumb, then quickly crossed the hall, pushing past the opposite door into a dimly lit room awash in that odd grey light that only comes from black and white video screens. He gave another okay and beckoned them over.

Horace took the knife away from Fred's neck and hustled him across the hall. Frank followed after, closing the kitchen door behind him. If he believed Fred, the only other people in the house were LaRouche, one more guard, and a maid.

Well, the screens should give them a better idea.

"Okay kid," Horace said. "Show us what all you can do with these things." Gently but firmly, he pushed Fred down into an exotic, high-backed contraption that resembled a spaceship cockpit more than an office chair. All mesh and control rods.

It looked comfortable. Frank would love to sit down and take a break for a week or so.

In his command seat, Fred straightened a little. He closed both hands into fists a few times, loosening his fingers. His knuckles crackled and popped, then he woke the sleeping monitors, one after the other.

The chair sat in front of a curved panel which sported eight thirty-inch flat-panel screens. Four of them showed the yard, the scenes moving from left to right and back again as the cameras panned. Frank saw no signs of blood or bodies, which was a relief. Nothing on tape to come out in any trials that might crop up.

One camera showed the street, presumably in front of the gate. No traffic, no people, just one big sedan cruising slowly down the lane. The skinny guy inside might have been asleep for all the attention he gave his surroundings.

The other three showed different rooms. A den that looked more like a safari park, the front hallway, and an old-fashioned, dark-paneled study. The study held over-stuffed chairs, bookcases lined with heavy volumes from floor to ceiling, a massive, darkly-varnished desk...

And LaRouche. But no Yvonne. Frank realized at that moment he'd been hoping in the back of his head that Fred lied about Kulish. No such luck, apparently. No second guard, either.

Shit.

CHAPTER 23

Frank felt it happen.

The old coldness crept in, like it used to back when he hurt people for a living. Numbed detachment flowed from his head down to his feet. He felt his face go flat, his eyelids dropping halfway. He straightened, back stiff and hands relaxed at his sides.

Showtime.

"How you want to play it, Boss?" Horace said, the usual humorous edge gone from his voice. His old friend was all business. He could read Frank like a book, and probably felt the same changes in his own body right now.

Frank didn't answer. Instead, he tapped Fred on the shoulder.

"Stand up, kid," he said. "Nice and slow. Look at me."

"Hey, mister," Fred said, getting shakily to his feet. "I did everything you said. Please don't hurt—"

"It's okay, Fred," Frank said, stepping back to give the boy a little room. "Plans have changed. We're not going to tie you up any more."

"We're not?" Horace asked.

"No," Frank said, still looking at Fred.

"We're going to let you leave," he said. "But you have to leave *now*. Go on, go where ever you go when you're not working. Forget everything about us. Can you do that?"

"'Cause if you don't, we're sure gonna remember you," Horace said, patting him kindly on the cheek.

"Sure," Fred said, brightening a little. "Sure I can. You bet! Thank you!" He started toward the hallway and his freedom.

Yakov held his arm across the door, blocking Fred's escape. The young man stopped, eyebrows drawn up, forehead wrinkled, his smile sagging a little. He had to be confused as all get out right now.

"I wish to apologize to you," Yakov said, fishing in his pocket and pulling out a twenty dollar bill. He tucked it into Fred's left-hand pants pocket. "I promised to make you a new lunch. But we have no time, so I will purchase your lunch instead. Is it fair with you?" He dropped his arm and opened the door.

That jerky, rapid-fire nod reappeared.

"Oh, sure," Fred said, a dashboard bobblehead on a bumpy road. "Plenty fair. I won't tell anyone. I promise. Thanks. Thanks a lot!" He left the room, turning right and running for the back door, nearly tripping over all the gratitudes spewing from his mouth.

Frank turned back to the screens, only vaguely registering Fred opening and then shutting the rear door. A few seconds later, an engine fired up and faded as the boy took them up on their offer.

Yvonne was gone. With Kulish, by all accounts a sex

slaver. Was he the one LaRouche had tried to send her to when she decided to leave him?

Why the hell had Frank listened when she told him to wait before coming after her?

He wanted to go find her right now. Wade in on Kulish with the sun at his back, guns blazing in a righteous bloodbath.

Only he wasn't righteous. He was currently a shylock, formerly a kneecapper and troubleshooter. Time to stop thinking with his smaller brain and approach this as a job.

On the screen, Yvonne's ex sat at the desk, going through papers, sorting them from one pile to another. He gave no sign he knew anything was amiss in his little world. Probably it never occurred to him that he might be in danger in his own castle.

"Come on guys," Frank said. "I...*we* need to get Yvonne away from Kulish, but I don't want to leave this shitbird in our six."

The stamp at the bottom of LaRouche's screen read *Q3 - 2 FLOOR EAST.* So he was upstairs. Good to know; at least they had a start.

The three of them turned left up the hallway and crept along, eyes and ears open and straining. Nothing beyond the normal subliminal voice of any inhabited house. Air hissed from vents. Window glass ticked as the sun moved across the sky. The washing machine beeped as the sloshing cut out.

Frank barely heard his and Horace's feet. Yakov might as well be a ghost. They made as much noise as a shadow on carpet.

At the end of the hall, the tack-o-rama den stretched

away to the left. Naked women on canvas and bits of dead animal climbed the walls nearly fifteen feet to a vaulted cathedral ceiling painted with zodiac constellations. To the right, a majestic blondwood staircase curved upward in a graceful half-spiral, the upper end opening on a small landing with an arch leading deeper into the second story.

The trio crept up the stairs. The landing led to a short hallway ending in a tall, mahogany door covered with carved dragons. To their left, sunlight poured through a set of closed French doors. No guard, no maid, no LaRouche.

From below, a shrill, piercing scream erupted from the direction of the kitchen.

Well, they knew where the maid was at least.

With no further need to sneak, Frank ran to the larger door, leveled the shotgun, and pulled the trigger. Splinters flew as the heavy lock disappeared. Up close, the birdshot might as well be a solid slug.

He kicked the door open and the three burst into the room.

Behind the desk, LaRouche struggled to stand. Frank raised the shotgun and shook his head.

The old man's shoulders slumped. He sat back, placed his hands on the blotter, palms down.

"Welcome to my home, Mr. Powers," LaRouche said, a wry smile lifting the corner of his mouth. "Are all my men dead?"

"All the ones we met," Frank said. Maybe not true, but fuck him. "Where's Yvonne?"

"My wife, you mean?" LaRouche asked. "*Mrs.* LaRouche? Why do you care?" His gaze flicked past Frank's right shoulder.

Frank spun around just as Horace slammed into him from the side.

LaRouche threw himself sideways.

A shotgun boomed in the hall.

Horace grunted as his shirt twitched.

A speckled pattern appeared in the wall beside the desk, but the desk itself was unmarked.

Horace fell, red blooming down his back.

"Ace!" Frank yelled. He scrambled to his knees, waving the shotgun back and forth, looking for the shooter.

Yakov shouted something foreign and threw one of the heavy Japanese tools down the hall. Frank heard the impact of metal on bone. Yakov ran from the room, following his weapon.

A scraping sound caught Frank's attention. He got to his feet, went behind the desk where LaRouche was trying to pull himself up.

Frank helped him out by grabbing his throat, jerking him to his feet, and throwing him back in his chair.

Various sounds better left unidentified came from the hall, then Yakov reappeared.

"Taken care of?" Frank asked. Yakov nodded.

"Watch this one, but don't hurt him. Yet."

He and Yakov traded places. Frank knelt by Horace, whose arms and legs moved weakly.

"You okay, Boss?" Horace whispered.

"I'm fine, Ace," Frank said, pulling Horace's shirt up to see a cluster of red dots running from his neck to his waist.

Small dots. Birdshot. Wide spread.

He'd be okay. Just fine.

"How you doing, buddy?"

"I hurt like hell," his oldest, best friend said. "Sorry I ain't gonna be much help no more."

"Shut up, you old fart," Frank said. "Yakov's going to take you to get patched up. I'll finish here and see you in a while."

"Sure, boss," Horace said. "Sure."

CHAPTER 24

AFTER THEY'D USED LAROUCHE'S SHIRT AND PANTS TO TIE the old man to his desk chair, Yakov agreed to take Horace to a friendly hospital. He gave Frank his cell number, then bent down and lifted Horace with no visible effort.

Horace would be fine. He was in good hands. None of the tiny wounds looked bad. The combination of distance, lightweight shot, and sawed-off barrel meant the pellets hadn't penetrated too deeply.

Frank kept telling himself that.

Meanwhile, Yvonne was still out there somewhere.

Frank watched Yakov as the foreign-born soldier carried away a man he'd just met and owed nothing. He stepped over the dead guard and went down the stairs without slowing, without hurrying.

Horace will be okay, Frank told himself. He's a tough old bastard. He'll be fine.

So would Yvonne. She could handle herself, no matter how rough things got.

Frank wrenched his attention back to the matter at hand.

He shut the ruined door and shoved one of the heavy chairs against it, just in case Fred had missed anyone, then went to LaRouche. He dropped the shotgun on the desk and pulled the polished brass syringe from his coat pocket.

"We were talking about Yvonne," Frank said. He took off his belt and wrapped it around LaRouche's bicep, waiting for a vein or two to pop.

"She isn't heah," LaRouche said, his Boston showing. "Kulish took her, you know that."

"He took her or you gave her away? Or sold her?"

"What difference does it make, ya bastahd?" LaRouche said. "He's got her now and that's that. I didn't have any choice."

"Where?"

"I can't tell you," LaRouche said. "I don't know."

"You ever heard the word agonist?" Frank asked, pointing the needle skyward, pressing the plunger until a dark stream squirted from the tip.

"I've heard of your scam," LaRouche said. "Everyone has. No one's met anyone you've used it on. Weird, huh?"

"True," Frank admitted, sliding the sharp needle into LaRouche's arm. "This probably isn't an agonist. What do you think?" He shot the entire load home. "This is for Horace. We'll let Kulish pay for Yvonne."

Immediately, LaRouche's skin flushed. Beads of sweat appeared on his upper lip and forehead.

"I can't tell you where she is, Mr. Powers," LaRouche said again, a slight quiver in his voice. He breath coming a little faster now.

"Here's the deal, you prick," Frank said, voice still quiet and calm. "You tell me where Kulish is, and I mean right fucking now, and I'll give you the antidote. You've got about ten minutes I'd say. Maybe less. Hard to tell." He sat on the desk, crossed his arms, and waited.

LaRouche's eyes were wide, growing bloodshot. The man's pulse beat heavily in his scrawny neck. A vein on his forehead throbbed. Sweat rolled down his face, chest, and arms.

LaRouche licked his lips. "If I tell you," he finally said, voice flat-out shaking now, "will you deal with him and not me? Can we make a deal to leave each other alone in the future?"

"Sure," Frank said. "In fact..."

He found a blank sheet of paper and a pen. He scooted LaRouche closer to the desk so he could see Frank writing his usual two line contract.

In return for Kulish's current whereabouts, Frank Powers will never interfere with or harm Quentin LaRouche again.

In return for this consideration, Quentin LaRouche guarantees to never bother Frank Powers again.

Frank scrawled his signature and left the paper on the desk.

"I trust you to do the right thing," Frank said. "Now where are they?"

LaRouche swallowed. "By the airport," he said, panting now. "Redland Imports. Please, Mr. Powers."

"How many guys?"

"Ten or fifteen, probably," LaRouche said. "Depends on who he has out on the streets."

"Okay!" Frank said, clapping his hands. "Thank you for helping me save your wife."

"The antidote?" LaRouche said.

"Can't do it, pal," Frank said.

"Money," LaRouche said. "Bottom drawer. Couple

hundred thousand." More veins stood out in his neck and face. Frank could see his heart beating, trying to jump from his chest.

The money was in a thick manila envelope. Frank counted out one hundred twenty-five thousand, the balance of his fee, and put the rest back. He didn't feel bad about it. LaRouche had gotten Yvonne back, after all.

"Please!" LaRouche gasped, eyes wide and blood red. "You said you wouldn't hurt or interfere—"

"I said 'again.' And I won't. I won't interfere to cause you further harm, or to save your worthless life."

LaRouche's red eyes widened even more, pupils starting to shrink.

"Antidote," he whispered, as close to begging as he could still manage.

Frank slowly shook his head.

"I lied. I don't have an antidote."

Frank sat on the desk, wiping his prints from the Browning, and watched Quentin LaRouche die.

CHAPTER 25

Frank dragged the three dead guards into the kitchen, opened the gas on the cooktop and oven, lit the candles on the small table, and left. He didn't hear any sirens, so the maid hadn't called 911.

He hoped not, anyway. He hoped no one arrived before the gas did its work.

Yakov had taken the car, so Frank hoofed it through the woods as far as he could. When he ran out of forest, he hit the empty sidewalks until he got to a busy convenience store where he could be incognito for a while.

Frank called the only number he could think of. The beat of house music assaulted his ear, along with the now-familiar accent.

"Yes?" Boris said.

"Busy?"

"I believe you are about to answer that question for me."

"I hate to tell you," Frank said. "You're unemployed."

"Will my employer be calling me again?"

"No, I'm afraid not. But *his* employer might be agitated."

"Very well," Boris said. "Tell me where I may find you."

Frank gave him the address, then told Boris what he'd heard from LaRouche. Boris sounded neither surprised nor happy.

"Infiltrating warehouses is very difficult," Boris said. "Too many unknowns. Too many places for people to conceal themselves."

"True," Frank said. "So how about it?"

"I will meet you at your office. I will call Yakov to pick you up."

"I'll call him," Frank said. "He's busy at the moment. Are you bringing any more people?"

"I think no," Boris said. "I do not wish to give Kulish more warning than he already has."

"Great," Frank said, and clicked off.

He called Yakov next. He confirmed Horace was in the care of Dr. Clayton at Piedmont Hospital. The same doctor who'd given him the BS agonist story he used on people like Lawrence Bradshaw.

A good doc. One of the best. Horace was going to be okay.

He told Yakov where to pick him up, disconnected the call, and leaned against the warm bricks. His mind ran like a squirrel in a cage, fretting about Yvonne and Horace.

At least he knew where Horace was and how he was doing. He knew nothing about Yvonne's situation. He had to go get her. Now.

Yakov, Frank, and Boris. Three against ten or fifteen. Maybe more. Bad odds.

Time to collect on an offer. He took a card from his pocket, dialed the number.

"What?" Marcus Kaplan said loudly, speaking over the

noise of loud dance music and drunken catcalls that filled The Jaguar, day and night.

"I need your help," Frank said, as Yakov pulled up in the rented Audi.

Frank told Kaplan about LaRouche and Kulish as he and Yakov sped toward Frank's office.

"We're going to end this," Frank said. "At least this chapter. I need you and Peterson."

"I'll come," Kaplan said. "But not Peterson. I'm leaving him here to watch out for the girls, in case...well, in case of trouble."

Better than nothing.

"Okay," Frank said. "Meet me at my office."

He gave the address and ended the call. Yakov stared straight ahead as he drove, silent.

"Horace will be well," Yakov said finally. "The doctor says there is no major damage. Tomorrow he will leave the hospital."

"Thank you, Yakov," Frank said. "Thank you for taking care of him."

"I do not wish that harm comes to him," Yakov said. "Or to you. I hope for all of us a quiet death in bed. Many years from now."

In spite of everything, Frank laughed. "You and me both, buddy," he said. "You and me both."

They rode in a more relaxed silence, arriving at the office before either Boris or Kaplan. The parking lot was still empty, except for the Audi and the panel truck with the Liebowitz Exterminators logo. The two who'd come in the truck should still be here. The exterminators exterminated.

The truck might come in handy.

Frank sent Yakov to take care of the two goons still

gagged and tied in the storage room. They'd have to deal with the bodies, but playing nice time was well over.

While Yakov did the necessary, Frank unlocked the door with the high voltage sign, revealing his private firearms cabinet. He ignored the pistols and shotguns, instead taking a well-cared for World War II vintage M1 rifle, plus a green satchel full of military hardball ammunition in eight-round clips.

Yakov came back in, wiping his hands in paper towels. "It is done," he said.

"Good. Thank you." Frank handed one of the Steyrs to Yakov. "Know how to use it?"

Yakov answered by popping the magazine, locking the bolt, examining the piece.

"It is a fine weapon," he said, snapping the magazine back in place and chambering a round.

They both spun as the outer door opened, relaxing when Boris came in. Kaplan followed close behind, eyes boring holes through Boris.

"You're working with this clown?" Kaplan said to Frank. "He's one of LaRouche's."

"No, he's not," Frank said. "He's as much of a white hat as we are, whatever that says."

Frank introduced Kaplan to Yakov, then turned the floor over to his huge guest.

"What do you know about Kulish's setup at his warehouse, Boris?"

"We know he has a dozen or so men there at all times," Boris said. "They will be armed with machine pistols, most likely. Collateral damage is not something which troubles the man."

"We've got two machine guns, a rifle, a couple of shotguns, and a few pistols in the cabinet over there," Frank said. "Can we get more?"

"Don't look at me," Kaplan said. "I've got my Walther, but I only carry a couple of mags."

"I have access to LaRouche's caches," Boris said. "However, I am sure his organization has heard of the unfortunate explosion at his residence. It was quite spectacular."

"We can pick up what we need at the warehouse," Frank said. "Dead men won't miss their guns."

They ordered pizza and planned their approach while they ate. The strategy wasn't complicated, given how little they knew. Kulish knew they were coming, but had no way to know how many or with what.

The sun finally went down. It was time. Frank stood and slung the M1.

"Let's go."

CHAPTER 26

FRANK DROVE THE CROTCHETY PANEL VAN TO THE AIRPORT, exiting at the Air Cargo section. Boris, Yakov, and Kaplan rode in the back, doing their final weapons check.

Boris told Frank where to turn, and soon he saw a typical air freight building with warehouse in back and offices up front. *Redland Imports* blazed above the entrance in glowing scarlet letters four feet tall.

The parking lot held no vehicles.

Frank drove to the next facility and parked. The weeds growing through the cracked pavement plus the boards over most of the windows meant no security guards.

He hoped, anyway.

The four men got out, stretched, and moved toward Kulish's place, bent low, trotting in a zig-zag pattern toward a chain link fence. Low hedges on either side partially masked the fence.

Boris and Kaplan carried the Steyrs, Frank had his M1, and Yakov had his Japanese choppers and a set of heavy-duty wire cutters. He also had a .357 revolver tucked in his belt, but Frank figured his new friend would be armed with something more shootable before much longer.

A quick check of the empty lot showed no movement. In less than a minute, Yakov snipped enough of the fence for them all to slip through. They hunkered down, peering through the foliage at the side of the warehouse. A steel entry door flanked the bigger loading bay shutters.

Nothing there. No guards, no people. Light came through the windows, but the frosted glass hid whoever might be in there.

Shit.

"Okay," Frank whispered. "I'll try to bring them out. Boris, you and Kaplan lay down suppressive fire on either side. Short bursts. Don't waste ammo until we get more."

The two gunners nodded and crept to either side of their guardian hedge. As cover, it wasn't much against bullets, but you can't have everything.

Frank rose enough to sight on the smaller door's window. He squeezed the trigger. A sharp report and bright muzzle flash destroyed the nighttime peace and quiet.

The tinkle of broken glass was immediately lost in the yells of those inside. Frank swung the barrel toward the front entrance, figuring no one would be stupid enough to come through a door with a fresh bullet hole in the window.

Worked like a charm.

Two men in suits came through the glass lobby doors, followed by a wiry, dark-haired creep in black jeans and a leather jacket. All three carried stubby automatic pistols, Steyrs matching those carried by Boris and Kaplan. Behind them came an older guy in a rent-a-cop uniform, holding a revolver in one hand and a radio in the other.

"Short bursts to the sides," Frank whispered again.

Boris and Kaplan squeezed off a few rounds each. Sparks flew from the asphalt and ricocheting bullets whined through the night. Both men rolled a few yards to the sides and lay flat.

The goons did just what Frank wanted. They bunched together, firing wildly toward where gunsmoke still hung in the heavy air.

Frank lined them up, then fired once. Twice. Three times.

The first copper-jacketed bullet cut through the leading suit-wearer's torso like butter, taking the short security guard behind him in the neck. The other two hadn't been close enough together, but Frank had no trouble dropping them individually.

Yakov was on the run before the last body hit the pavement, making sure none of them were merely wounded. He grabbed two of their pistols and sprinted to wait by the door Frank had blown the window out of.

Frank, Boris, and Kaplan ran to meet him. Yakov fired into the lockplate and kicked the door open. They all entered at a crouched run, heading toward the inner door and out of the open loading area.

Frank stopped and looked around the cavernous room, noting all the wooden crates. He couldn't read the Cyrillic markings, but the rope handles and stenciled letters said military.

Boris and Kaplan watched the door as Frank and Boris opened a few of the smaller boxes. Ammunition, spare magazines, and...

Bingo.

Packed in wood shavings and sawdust were a couple-dozen *limonka* hand grenades. They resembled old US Army pineapple grenades, but with a long brass fuse sticking out the top.

Fun stuff. What to do, what to do?

Frank took four of the heavy grenades and handed them to Boris before taking four more for himself. He wasn't sure *how* they would come in handy, but he knew the right moment would reveal itself.

As much as he hated to, Frank laid his trusty M1 behind one of the stacks and caught the 9-millimeter pistol Yakov tossed his way. No room to maneuver a rifle in here. At least he could grab a few extra magazines for the handgun from the stash they'd found.

Yakov stood by the inner door, hand patting the air as he pressed his ear against the gray metal. Frank and Boris joined him and Kaplan, all waiting until Yakov flashed a circle of thumb and finger.

Frank tried the knob. Locked, of course. And no keyhole, just a small chrome box with a standard 12-button keypad.

Yakov tapped Frank's shoulder. He stepped aside, and Yakov went to work.

It was beautiful to watch.

He pulled a flat pouch filled with fine tools from his chest pocket, selecting a tiny flat-bladed screwdriver and some sort of probe. In two seconds, the box's cover was off.

Yakov took a small circuit board from another pocket, one which trailed three fine wires. He clipped the leads to various bits of the lock gizmo, then tapped 1-2-3-4 on the keypad.

A soft click, and he turned the knob easily.

The door opened into the middle of a hallway which

ran the width of the building. To the right, weak light came in through the glass-fronted lobby. To the left, the corridor turned and continued. No way to know what was up there.

Except for the leather-jacketed goon who came sprinting around the corner, grease gun in hand.

A silver blur shot past Frank's head.

The goon dropped his gun and grabbed his throat, where a black-wrapped knife handle had sprouted.

Boris and Kaplan ran to finish the guard. Frank turned to Yakov, eyebrow raised.

"Horace was kind enough to lend me his knives," Yakov said with a shrug.

Frank started to reply, but the sound of more running feet cut him off. He shot past his two friends and the dead guard to the corner, pulling the pin on one of the Russian grenades.

"Fire in the hole!" he yelled, throwing the grenade around the corner and sprinting back to the others. They all hit the ground.

Two more guards appeared. They stopped, raised their weapons, then slammed sideways into the wall as the grenade roared and sprayed shrapnel through their bodies.

Hopefully their buddies had been behind them.

Above them, dust filled the air from shredded drywall, but Frank and the others hadn't caught any flying bits of metal.

"Which way?" Frank asked Boris as they rose.

"Through the lobby, I think," Boris replied. "I for one would not go where a grenade just exploded, and I do not wish to be surprised from behind. I believe the time for automatic weapons is done, as we do not know where Miss

Yvonne is." He and Kaplan dropped their heavy Steyr machine guns and drew their pistols.

Frank and his crew ran down the hall to the right, cutting through the empty reception area and up the only other corridor, throwing doors open as they went, clearing the area.

As they approached an intersection where a hall cut to the left, three more goons ran out right in front of them.

There was no time to think. All seven men started firing wildly. Bullets whizzed past Frank's ears, and he felt a line of heat in his left bicep as a shot grooved his arm.

The shooting lasted only a few seconds, although it seemed more like minutes. Kulish's men were all down, only one of them stirring weakly.

"Anybody hit?" Frank asked, looking at Boris, who shook his head. Yakov's left ear bled from a crescent-shaped wound. Frank turned to Kaplan.

Who was sliding down the wall, looking down at his chest where pinkish, frothy blood bloomed around a small black hole just above his diaphragm. Lung shot.

"Kaplan!" Frank yelled. He grabbed Kaplan under the arms and eased him down until he sat on the polished tiles.

Frank wished he had something to say. He gripped Kaplan's hands as the dying man's face turned up to his.

But there were no profound words. Kaplan coughed blood, and spoke in a gasping voice as wind whistled in and out of the hole in his chest.

"This...sucks..."

Frank sat with him as his eyes emptied and his head slumped forward.

Shit.

CHAPTER 27

"Come, my friend," Boris said. "We must finish this now. We will pay our respects when everything is done."

Frank looked at Kaplan's face one last time, then took the dead man's pistol and rose, wincing when his knees popped.

He was getting too old for this.

A large, heavy wooden door blocked the end of the hall. They approached it slowly, guns aimed forward.

Frank heard nothing.

Nothing except the distant wail of sirens, getting louder.

"Cover me," he said. How many cheesy movies and TV shows had he seen where someone spouted the same line? He hadn't covered Kaplan at—

Get outta yer goddamn head.

Frank reached out with his left hand and threw the door open. He saw three...no, four people inside before more gunfire spat toward him.

All three hit the deck, firing upward at the gunmen. The one on the left went down almost immediately.

Another dropped his gun after a few more shots and raised his hands over his head.

The third man sat behind the desk, a woman in his lap and a Beretta in his hand.

But not pointing at Frank, Boris, or Yakov.

A single shot rang out, and the man trying to surrender went down in a heap, a nice neat hole punched through both sides of his skull.

Frank barely noticed.

Kulish had a lap full of Yvonne. She wasn't struggling, but she didn't look happy either.

"What kept you, hon?" she said, her voice light but her eyes damp.

"Sorry, Yvie," Frank said. "Fastest I could get here."

Kulish got up, putting Yvonne on her feet but holding her body in front of his. For some reason, she wore a red sequin cocktail gown and tall heels.

Kulish himself stood nearly as tall as Frank, but instead of his and Boris's thick muscles, Kulish was slender, with sharp, hawkish features. Salt-and-pepper hair swept back from a high brow, and a pencil-thin mustache rode his upper lip.

"What's going on?" Frank said. "Did we interrupt a party?"

"There will indeed be a party," Kulish said. "One which Miss LaRouche here will attend, but you will not. Nor will the traitor Boris, or the other one you brought."

The pistol in his hand now pointed directly at Frank's face.

"There are three of us," Frank said. "You can't win."

"Perhaps not," Kulish said. "But you may lose. If you

attempt to shoot me, this poor young woman will be the first to fall."

"Don't you hear the sirens? They've got to be right outside." Which was true. Frank wondered why he heard no running feet or barked commands. "So now what?"

Why weren't Boris and Yakov doing anything?

"If you wish the woman to live," Kulish said, "you will drop your weapons and kick them into the hall."

Shit, shit, shit! What the hell to do?

"Would you please kill this asshole?" Yvonne asked. Kulish's arm tightened and she gasped, but didn't look away from Frank's face.

"Sorry, Yvie," Frank said. "Some rescue, huh?"

He let his pistol fall to his side. Yakov did likewise. Boris still held his on Kulish and Yvonne, unwavering.

In the silence, Yvonne sighed.

"Do I have to do everything myself?"

Yvonne lifted her left leg and stomped down on Kulish's foot with one ridiculously long heel. Frank heard the sharp snap of bone.

At the same time, she jerked sideways. Kulish fired once, but was off balance and the bullet tore into the wall above the door.

At nearly the same instant, Boris squeezed his own trigger. Frank saw Kulish's jacket twitch between his right arm and collarbone, then the Russian's arm went dead.

He let go of his remaining hold on Yvonne to clutch his ruined shoulder. She ran to Frank, who held his arms open to receive her embrace.

She ducked behind him instead.

"Could you please shoot that rat bastard for me?" she said.

"No," Boris said. "He may not."

Frank, Yvonne, and Yakov looked at the giant Ukrainian, who stared at Kulish with flat, emotionless eyes.

"Gregor Kulish," he began. The rest was in Russian and Frank couldn't follow, but he knew a verdict and sentencing when he heard them.

"You okay, Yvie?" Frank said, turning and embracing the cause of all his trouble.

"I'm fine," she said, her words muffled in his chest as she hugged him back. Hard. "He was going to take me with him. Break me and keep me for a pet, he said." She shuddered.

Behind them, Boris stopped talking. Kulish began to speak, his voice hard and angry.

Two quick gunshots cut his reply off.

"Nicely done," someone said from the hall. Frank and Yvonne looked around and saw a short, thin man in a black suit and tie.

"Special Agent Jerry Wood," the new arrival said. "United States FBI." He held open his credential wallet as though they could read it from several yards away. Frank recognized the face he'd been seeing through windshields and windows. The face that up until now had worn black aviator sunglasses.

"Mr. Wood," Boris said, holstering his pistol. "It is most good to see you again."

"Pleasure's all mine," Wood said. "We all done here?"

"Say, Boris," Yvonne said. "If you don't mind me asking, what the hell's going on?"

"Why nothing," Wood said. "Nothing at all. We're just here responding to reports of suspicious activity. Looks like an illegal arms deal went bad, judging from all the hardware in the loading bay. The bad guys must've disagreed on terms and shot each other up. That about cover it, Kovalenko?"

"Indeed," Boris said. "Most unfortunate you were not in time to apprehend the others, but who knows? Perhaps both groups killed each other."

Frank looked from one smiling face to the other.

"That's it?" he said. "You feebies don't care what happened here?"

"Don't think that, Mr. Powers," Wood said. "We are very happy to have gun-runners and pimps out of action. We just couldn't do anything ourselves without a warrant or probable cause, and Kulish has, that is to say *had,* lots of friends. You're bleeding, by the way."

Frank saw that his sleeve had turned red from the graze he'd taken. He tore a strip from his shirt and wound it around his bicep.

"Can't tell you how much I appreciate you boys stepping in when we were getting tied up, beaten, and shot at."

"And ruin all your future stories?" Wood said, one corner of his mouth twitching upward. "Perish the thought, Mr. Powers. Besides, we don't know what's really been happening, do we? Not officially, at least."

"Mr. Wood and I have worked together on this for several weeks," Boris said. "As I am not technically in this country, I can do certain things he cannot. As can you, Mr. Powers."

"I get it," Frank said. "You played me for a fool and got me to help you take these guys out."

"Not at all," Boris said. "You simply got entangled with Mr. and Mrs. LaRouche, and I saw an opportunity. I and my countrymen thank you. My country women as well, once we have all of them freed from the vice dens."

"About that," Frank said. "A bunch of girls are stuck in a basement near—"

"Already taken care of," Wood said. "We were in there shortly after LaRouche's untimely gas leak."

"You helped do the world a great service," Boris added. "More than you think."

"What's that supposed to mean?" Frank said.

Wood smiled. "Ask your brother Bill, sometime," he said. "He can fill you in." With that, the little man turned and left.

"How about that?" Yvonne said, giggling and chucking Frank under the chin. "You're a bona fide hero, sugar!"

CHAPTER 28

IT WAS TEN-THIRTY THE NEXT MORNING BEFORE FRANK managed to get to Horace's hospital room. His arm felt stiff and swollen, but the pills Doc Clayton had given him kept the pain away.

He asked the desk nurse in Recovery and got the right room number. He walked in just as Yakov opened the door from the inside. He and Horace were both laughing. They stopped when Frank came in.

Yakov, normally stoic as an old Indian brave, actually looked flustered. He shot quick glances between Frank and Horace, then moved past Frank.

"I will get the car," he said over his shoulder. "Please to meet me downstairs."

Frank watched him walk toward the elevators, then turned to stare at Horace, eyebrows raised.

Horace smiled serenely, looking like a tomcat with an alibi.

He wore his battered old cowboy hat with a new purple bandanna Frank hadn't seen before, but still wore his hospital johnnie.

"How you doing, Ace?" Frank asked.

"Oh, I'm fine," Horace said. "Gotta wear loose clothes for a few days, but the doc got all the pepper outta me. Help me get into that wheelchair, would you Boss?"

"Oooookay," Frank said. He took his old friend's arm and helped him over to the waiting chair. Horace looked fine, but he moved slow and careful. Birdshot on top of the beating he'd taken had added up for sure. "Who's taking you home? Me or..."

"Ol' Yakov offered me a ride," Horace said, his voice so innocent Frank was instantly wary. "He said it was the least he could do after I loaned him my knives."

"Is that all?" Frank said. "Just knives? And what happened to 'jackoff'?"

"Oh, he ain't so bad," Horace said. "He's real sweet once you get to know him."

The way he said sweet made it clear they were getting to know each other pretty well.

Frank settled Horace in the wheelchair, released the brakes, and started pushing him down the hall.

"How's Yvie?" Horace said. "She gonna be okay? Yakov told me what all went down last night."

"She'll be fine," Frank said with complete sincerity. "She'll outlive all of us, laughing all the way."

"She thank you proper for comin' to get her?" Horace said, leering up at Frank.

"Let's just say I have no complaints," Frank said, trying to sound as smug as Horace.

The elevator let them out on the ground floor, and Frank wheeled Horace to the curb where Yakov waited.

He didn't tell Horace about the note that shared his bed when he woke up an hour ago. A note that thanked him for the rescue, apologized for the fifty grand he'd be missing, and promised she'd get in touch as soon as she decided how she felt about the future.

It hurt to see that note, but it was Yvonne Rudabaugh all over, and more than she'd left him with the last time.

"Boss? Hey, Boss!"

Frank finally registered Horace's voice. "Sorry, Ace. Lot on my mind."

"There should be," Horace said as Yakov helped him from the chair into his car. "It's Saturday, and still no word from Lawrence Bradshaw. You need to go see the tubby little twerp and straighten him out." He slammed the door, and he and Yakov drove away, leaving Frank standing alone.

Shit.

Frank went to his own car, planning how to separate Bradshaw from the money the man owed him. In spite of himself, he started to whistle, finding a new strut in his step. Life would be back to normal, however he chose to define the word.

And life was good.

ABOUT JASON

Jason A. Adams grew up a military brat, a life that exposed him to many places, people from around the world, and a lifetime curiosity that informs his fiction.

Jason is the author of one novella, and many short stories based in and around the Virginia coalfields he lives in and loves. He currently lives on a forest mountain with his beautiful wife, Kari Kilgore, also a writer of many wonderful stories.

You can keep up with upcoming fiction from both Jason and Kari, their travel adventures, and whatever else strikes their fancy at www.jasonadams.info, www.karikilgore.com, and www.spiralpublishing.net.

news@jasonadams.info

facebook.com/Jason.A.Adams.2

ALSO BY JASON A. ADAMS

I hope you enjoyed reading *Agonist* as much as I enjoyed writing it.

Visit www.jasonadams.info and join the adventure for exclusive new fiction, my past and future travels, and whatever else strikes my fancy. Hope to see you there!

Mick of Malvern: Seeker for Hire (A Hard-Boiled Fairy Tale)

Sunlit Dispositions (A Hard-Boiled Space Opera)

To Catch a Thief (An Appalachian Gothic Tale)

"Our huntsman took Princess Ambrosia for a stroll
in the forest yesterday morning," the queen said.
"According to his report, someone struck him on the
head. When he came back to himself, she was
gone."

"And where is the huntsman?"

"The huntsman is no longer any concern,"
Gareth said, his voice cold and flat. "Her Majesty is
relying on you to correct his failure."

My dagger shrank into a needle. No point asking
what would happen if I couldn't bring her back.
Besides, this was an important case, for an
important client. An important *rich* client.

"I shall succeed or die," I said.

"We are well aware of that," the queen said.

I knew then it wasn't the princess' skin I needed
to save.